Elder Shelton –
It has been a pleasure working
with you in the stake mission.
With Love,
Boyd

Knife Thrower

KNIFE THROWER

A MORMON BOY AMONG THE PAWNEE

Boyd Richardson

Boyd Richardson

Covenant Communications, Inc.

Published by Covenant Communications, Inc.
American Fork, Utah

Copyright © 1994 by Boyd Richardson
All rights reserved

Printed in the United States of America
First Printing: March 1994

01 00 99 98 97 96 95 94   10 9 8 7 6 5 4 3 2 1

Library of Congress Cataloging-in-Publication Data

Richardson, Boyd, 194

   Knife Thrower

    p. cm.   '

ISBN 1-55503-683-X : $7.95

1. Fiction. 2. Historical Fiction. I. Title.

ACKNOWLEDGMENTS

I would like to express appreciation to my editors, JoAnn Jolley and Giles H. Florence, Jr., and to my talented illustrator, Owen Richardson. Special thanks also go to the Richardson family proofreaders—Calvin, Corey, James, Jilane, Kim, Margie, May, Michael, Niesha, and Todd—and to Karen Rima. I am grateful for their constant help and support during the completion of this project.

MISSOURI MOB

IT WAS THE DEAD OF NIGHT as I lay on my straw tick listening to the sounds in the darkness. Something had awakened me, though I wasn't sure what it was. Outside, the Missouri winter night was cold and crisp; not cold enough for the limbs to snap, but there were noises in the night that shouldn't have been there.

The cabin loft that did duty for my bedroom was not large enough for an adult to stand up in . . . me neither, though I was a boy of ten years and small for my age. My size had bothered me, because Papa is a big man, towering head and shoulders above most everyone 'cept maybe Joseph Smith, and Mama's a tall woman, too.

"You should be satisfied with the body the good Lord gave you," Mama had lectured when I complained of my short stature. "But chances are you'll grow. Neither your papa nor I got our growth 'til we reached our teenage years."

It came again, the noise that had awakened me. Someone or something was out there, beyond the walls of the cabin, moving in the night. Lifting my head slightly off the tick so I could catch the slightest sound, I held my breath, but all I heard were the low words of Papa and Mama, softly speaking as they lay in their bed in the room below me. Mama had been in bed for nearly a month, so sick she could hardly make it to and from the privy behind the cabin.

"We need to get more books for him. He's on his fourth reading of the Book of Mormon and the second reading of the Bible. You said you were going to borrow some books from Brother Pratt," Mama was whispering. I was a good reader, but had never read anything but the scriptures and Brother Phelps's newspapers.

"Brother Pratt was off with the brethren somewhere, so I didn't see him. Besides, it's unnatural for a boy Samuel's age to read so much. When he's not working, he should be pulling sticks or playing some childhood game."

"He likes to throw those throwing knives of yours . . . can hit a knot straight on every time."

"I know, Ma, but even that's unnatural. He's always by himself."

"You know that there aren't any boys his age around."

"Yes, I know it, Ma, but there's the gentile boys."

"You shouldn't talk that way, Pa. The gentile boys aren't fitting friends for our son. They take the Lord's name in vain reg'larly and are more heathen than the Lamanites! 'Sides, Samuel's sickly, and the gentile boys torment him no end."

The sound came again. Someone was out there for sure. I eased myself to my elbow, throwing off my covers and reaching for my shoes. I didn't like shoes, never wore shoes 'cept in the dead of winter. Adults wore shoes all summer, which was a puzzlement to me.

"Someone's out there," Papa was saying. He was getting dressed as I slid down the ladder from the loft, scarcely touching the rails.

Suddenly sparks flew from the fire that had been banked for the night. A brick tumbled from the fireplace and Mama yelled, "They're pulling down the chimney!"

The door burst open like a cork being popped from a bottle and along with a gust of northern wind two burly mobsters filled the door frame. A flintlock firearm was discharged with a spray of sparks, and Papa gave a grunt as the ball struck him in his stomach. Immediately the room filled with a shower of mobsters with blackened faces.

2

Mama screamed and tried to run to Papa, but a bearish mobster grabbed her, holding her from reaching Papa. "Murderer!" she screamed at the man who held the flintlock. "You are all cold-blooded murderers!"

"You heathen Mormonites are abolitionists!" he shouted.

"Jacob Foster!" Mama yelled as she was pushed to the door, "you think no one knows who you are 'cuz you stove-blacked your face! But I know you by your voice, and you're nothing but a cold-blooded murderer, no better than the imps in hell!"

As I was shoved out the door, out of the corner of my eye I saw Mama snag the corner of a quilt and draw it to her. In her flimsy nightclothes and with no shoes, the quilt was her only hedge against the winter cold.

A man was holding me, but he didn't seem to have his heart in the task. Other mobsters were looting our meager belongings, while the man holding me was losing out on all the action.

"Run!" Papa yelled as he cast an eye my direction. Being a big man, he was held securely by no less than half a dozen mobsters. With a wild fling, I pulled away and sprinted for the woods. My guard was either not up to following me, or he didn't have his heart in the chase.

As I neared the trees, I saw a house afire down the road a quarter mile, and supposed it belonged to Brother Savage. I glanced over my shoulder to our own home, and saw in the light of many torches that some mobsters were holding Mama and Papa, while others were pulling the logs apart that framed our cabin.

Papa was holding his stomach, and I knew he would be almighty sore once the infection set in. Tears gathered in my eyes, 'cause I knew that once you've been gut-shot, you're as good as dead . . . a slow, painful death, they say. That was the last I saw before I drifted into the safety of the trees.

All night I huddled in the forest. I was cold, but it wasn't for me that I feared. I was worried sick about Mama and Papa. Come first light in the morning, I timidly made my way back to the remains of our cabin. Everything had been broken or stolen.

I found the remains of my straw tick. When the mob pulled the cabin down, the loft where I slept had come down with the roof. Sliding my hand under the tick, I found Papa's throwing knives where I always kept 'em. One was in the little holster he had made for me, that fit in the center of my back between my shoulder blades, and the other one was in a belt sheath. The knives were Papa's, because no one can afford to give such fine steel knives to a boy. But Papa had been letting me use 'em so long that they were almost mine.

My heart was aching for Mama and Papa, but there were so many tracks in the snow that it seemed unlikely for a ten-year-old lad like myself to find Mama and Papa's tracks. If they were still alive, there were only three logical explanations: they had been captured, they had escaped, or they had been turned loose.

As I started down the road, every now and again I saw a barefoot footprint and guessed it might be Mama's. Yet most of the time I saw only boot prints. I didn't know if Papa had time to put on his boots, but if he had, chances were that he was carrying Mama. A mile along, I saw where a man had left the road and made for a dense stand of timber. They were the prints of boots like Papa's, and now and again I saw specks of blood in the white snow.

The snow crunched under my feet, and I was mighty careful. Yet by now I was sure I was following Papa.

"Samuel!" a male voice called. "We're over here!" It was Papa; I'd know the voice anywhere.

It took a minute to locate the source of the voice because they were well hidden, huddled together at the base of a tree. I made my way to them, and was taken aback by their appearance. Papa looked like death, grimacing with pain from the ball in his stomach.

I went to my knees, and he took me in his once-powerful arms and held me close. As he held me he rocked slightly, and I could feel heaves from his chest, as if he were stifling sobs.

"How's Mama?" I asked.

"She's sleeping, I think," he said. Gingerly he parted the quilt far enough so that we could see her face. She looked up at me through hot, hollow eyes, then slid out an arm to embrace me. Softly crying, she held me for a few minutes; then I felt a shiver go through her body as if she were cold.

"Will you strike a fire, son," Papa said, extracting a flint rock and a hunk of old steel from his pocket. He always kept them in his pocket, much like some men carry pocket knives. "Now that the soreness has set in, my strength is slipping."

I struck the fire, then set to work making a lean-to and a reflector. It was the first time I'd been warm since the mobbing.

"How did you get away from the mob?" I asked.

"They let us go, saying they didn't want to see us or any other Mormons in this part of Missouri again. They said they'd shoot on sight."

"Why do they hate us, Papa?"

"They say it's because we're abolitionists and Indian lovers, but I think it is because Mormons represent law and order and restrictions. A goodly portion of the old settlers came to Missouri 'cuz they couldn't abide civilized restrictions."

After I had made my parents as comfortable as I could, I set out to find help for them. I didn't find help, but I raided the corn bin of a farmer. Carrying as large an armload of cobs as I could, I made my way back to Mama and Papa.

No one responded when I hollered the camp, so I laid my corn in the snow and proceeded cautiously. Papa was sitting by the fire, holding Mama in his arms, but the fire wasn't much more than coals. As I approached, Papa looked up through red eyes.

"How's Mama?" I asked, sensing something was wrong.

"She has gone to live with Jesus," he replied.

I pulled the quilt aside, and looked into her open, lifeless eyes. Sinking to my knees, I threw my arms around her lifeless body. Inside I was crying, but outwardly there were no tears—only a growing hatred for the mob and all the Missourians. I even hated God and Brother Joseph.

Papa looked into my eyes, and didn't seem to like what he saw. "Don't blame God," he pleaded. "Your mother would have died anyway. She was a mighty sick woman. Still, I would have liked her last hours to be spent in her comfortable bed."

"I . . . I've got some food for you, Papa," I muttered, not knowing what else to say, "though it's only animal corn. I left it in the snow when I hollered the camp."

"Get it, son, an' we'll parch it in the coals."

I made my way to where I had left the corn, but on glancing down my back trail I was brought up short. Some mobsters were following my tracks in the snow.

"The Missourians are coming," I said breathlessly after I'd sprinted back to Papa. "They're not more than half a mile away."

"Guess they had second thoughts 'bout lettin' your ma and me go," he muttered, his forehead wrinkling in worry lines. "Run for it, Samuel!"

"I don't want to leave you, Papa!"

"Son," he said softy, "I'm dying. Even if I weren't, the mob can't allow me to live because I'd tell everyone they killed your ma by driving her out of her home in the dead of winter. So run, Samuel, and don't worry about me!"

"Where will I go?"

"To Brother Joseph, maybe your Uncle Jacob Harold, to anyone but the godless Missourians.

6

There was just time for one last embrace and a parting kiss on his rough cheek. Then I ran, but this time hot tears streamed down my cheeks, because I knew I was leaving Mama and Papa for good . . . and what does a ten-year-old boy know about making his own way in the world? Fifty feet away, I cast them one backwards glance. Papa was holding Mama as if she were alive. I could hear the mobsters making their way through the crunchy snow, but above their noisy floundering was Papa's hoarse voice singing, "Whispering Hope."

That was the last time I saw either of them. Years later when I inquired about them, nobody seemed to know a thing.

THE ESCAPE

I RAN, knowing it was impossible for me to hide my tracks in the snow. But mobsters are a lazy, cowardly lot, preferring to torment the helpless rather than to expend real energy. Yet when they said they'd shoot any Mormon they found on sight, I believed 'em, 'cuz Papa said that was the nature of mobsters. If the Mormons hadn't been around for them to torment, they would have found someone else: blacks, halfbreeds, Indians, anyone they perceived to be inferior to themselves.

I wanted to find the other Mormon refugees, but I didn't know where they'd gathered, if indeed they had gathered. Papa said Uncle Jacob was in New Orleans. He was a good man, according to Papa, 'cept Papa said he was given to "wine, women, and song," whatever that means.

As I ran, I wished for the corn I'd stolen for Mama and Papa, yet all my efforts had been for naught. I ran west, not because west was better than any other direction, but because the woods seemed denser to the west. When I tired of running I walked, or rather wandered. Nothing looked familiar. It wasn't that I was lost, as I knew my directions, but I was in new territory.

Come evening I wished for a fire, but had none. 'Course I could make fire by friction . . . all us boys knew how to do it, but it's mighty difficult in the winter when the wood is cold and ofttimes damp. And you have to have soft wood, too, something I hadn't collected as I wandered.

I slid my hands deep into my pockets and my fingers struck something hard. It was Papa's flint and steel that I'd neglected to return to him when I'd struck a fire for him and Mama. With trembling cold hands, I pulled the bark off a deadfall, forming the inner bark into a tinder nest, then struck a spark. With the fire going I huddled close, toasty warm on one side and freezing on the other. I'd have to construct a reflector if I were gonna be halfway comfortable all night.

Hunger gnawing at my ribs, I slept fitfully. This was wild country, given to occasional bears, gray wolves, and who knows what else.

The morning dawned gray and overcast, yet it was a little warmer. A red squirrel ventured down a tree. It was his last trip, 'cuz my throwing knife found him halfway down the trunk. I cleaned him and roasted him over my fire, tearing off hot chunks of juicy meat as he cooked. I couldn't eat fast, because my stomach seemed to have shrunk, so I ate slowly, savoring every mouthful. When the meat was gone, I looked at the bones longingly, then started gnawing at them.

In the distance I thought I heard the bellowing of a cow wanting to be milked. I tilted my head, straining for every sound. Again I heard the bellowing, from the west. "Perhaps I can steal some more corn," I thought. 'Course it all depended on whether the farmer had a dog or not. Many people had dogs, but this was freshly-settled land, and dogs were still scarce.

When I reached the farm I found it was on the bank of a wide river, which I took for the Missouri Platte. It was a tidy looking farm with a granary and a boat dock. A rowboat was resting upside down on two logs near the dock. With that rowboat, I thought, I could float all the way down to New Orleans and find Uncle Jacob. I'd heard tell it was warm down there all winter long. 'Course I'd rather find Brother Joseph, wherever he was, but I surely didn't know how. Some said he was in Far West, but I wasn't rightly sure where that was. Still my immediate need was warmth and food, and that rowboat looked like my ticket to prosperity. At least in New Orleans it would be warm.

All day I waited in hiding. Now and again I saw the farmer cross from the house to the barn and back. I was hungry, but couldn't find a second squirrel that wanted to venture out this time of year.

Come night, I crept out and began making my way toward the boat dock. When I reached the barn I slipped in, looking for the corn bin in the dark. Finding it, I stuffed my shirt full of cobs, then proceeded to the landing. While righting the boat and slipping it into the water, I thought I heard noise coming from the farmhouse, so I crawled into the boat, cast off, then lay concealed in the bottom as the boat drifted downstream.

Gradually I became aware that water was seeping into the bottom of the boat. It was too late to turn back, as I was already into the swift-moving portion of the river. With cupped hands I tried to bail out the water, and didn't do too badly.

The moon had sunk behind the clouds, so it was too dark to see the bank. Yet the river began to calm, so I suspected I was swinging back into shore. I kept casting my eyes to the left, hoping to catch a glimpse of anything that signaled dry land. As I bailed water, I just happened to look to the right and caught the silhouettes of trees along the bank, so I grabbed the oars and began to pull hard for the shoreline. I was already soaking wet, so when I neared shore I jumped into the water and began dragging the boat.

The little boat was a bad idea anyway, but all is well that ends well, they say. Yet I wondered, was all well? I was on the wrong side of the river, probably sandwiched somewhere between the Platte and the Missouri Rivers. Across the Platte there were occasional farms and ranches where I could steal corn, but here there was nothing. 'Course I could always recross . . . I'd done it once, and I could do it again.

Soaking wet and shivering uncontrollably, my first thoughts were for heat. Searching out a deadfall, I stripped some inner bark and made a tinder nest. Then I struck a spark the way I'd been doing all my life, and in no time I had a fire going using the river bank for a reflector, the way Papa had taught me. Wet as I was, I was still hot on one side and freezing on the other, so I built a second fire to balance out the heat. As I started to dry out I began to relax, and was soon asleep.

In the morning I parched my stolen corn. I never knew parched corn to be so tasty, and it felt good to have a full stomach. Then I went to my boat to see what could be done to seal the leaks. It wasn't there! How could I be so stupid as to not drag it farther ashore than I had?

I looked across the river, and just stood there with my mouth open. It was huge! In the darkness I must have floated into the Missouri River. Was I in the Indian Nation, or was I in Missouri? If in Missouri, was I above or below Independence? I recalled that the river north of Independence flowed west to east, but the river I was on was flowing southeast, so I guessed I was west of Independence, in Indian Territory.

I was in trouble, big trouble. Some Mormons had been teaching the Lamanites and said they were fine people, but it was for darn sure that I wasn't going to have anything to do with them, because in spite of the mobsters' opinion 'bout Mormons being Indian lovers, I was more scared of the Indians than the Missourians. A story was ofttimes repeated about a two-year-old girl in New England who had been the victim of Indian savagery. The heathens had lopped off both arms and legs and left the toddler to entertain them as she hobbled on stumps of legs and screamed herself to death. No, siree! It was okay to read about the Lamanites in the Book of Mormon, but that's where it ended!

What was I doing here, anyway? I was just a boy in a savage land. I should be home in our warm cabin with Mama and Papa. How could I get down to Uncle Jacob's in New Orleans—or even across the river, for that matter?

I sank to my knees and pleaded with God—the same God I'd hated a few days earlier. Maybe I still hated him, I don't know; but when you have only one person to talk to, and you shut that one person out, you have no one at all. But then maybe it didn't matter. Maybe I'd go and live with Jesus like Mama and Papa.

Like a blast of warm air on a cold night, I realized I didn't want to live with Uncle Jacob, nor did I want to run to Brother Joseph. I wanted to live with Jesus. Even the air temperature around me seemed warmer, and I thought I heard angels singing. Mama said someone from the spirit world always came and got you when you died, someone you knew who was dressed in white. I wondered who would come for me. Would it be Mama? I closed my eyes and recalled every feature of her face. Yes, I was ready, ready to live with Mama . . . and Jesus.

A COUGAR
IN THE WILDS

AT BEST, IT'S HARD to find food in the winter. I'd been taught about edible roots and herbs by my parents, and would have been taught even more had they lived. But with snow covering the ground, I didn't know where to start looking. I needed to wander to find food, but I also needed to stay put to use the fire as protection against predators.

To the south coyotes roamed the plains, and to the north the gray wolf was king. In the wooded areas, cougars and bears roamed, living on deer, antelope, and buffalo. I worried because food is scarce in the winter, and I didn't want to be the main course at a cougar's or bear's dinner. Of course grizzlies sleep during the winter, but according to Papa, the lazy cinnamon bear doesn't find himself a den and wakes up on cold nights. When he wakes he has to move about to keep from freezing, so he gets hungry and likes food that is easy to catch, such as a ten-year-old boy.

The second night after I had been stranded on the west bank, I heard something that sounded much like a big animal yawning, but it ended in a scream. At the time I didn't know that I was listening to the scream of a cougar, nor had I believed that all the imps in hell could make such a frightening sound. At first I was literally frozen with fear, then suddenly I was all arms and legs, building a second and a third fire. It was after dark, and I positioned myself in the center of the three fires, venturing out only for more firewood.

Repeatedly I checked my two throwing knives, one on my belt

and one in a sheath in the center of my back. Yet I was afraid that when the time came and I was actually facing a cougar or a bear, I would be so frozen with fear I couldn't kill the beast. Even worse, I might throw a knife at an animal and not kill him. Then the animal might run off with my knife in him to die someplace all alone, and I'd lose the knife.

I tried to sleep, but fear kept me awake. Then suddenly they were there: two eyes in the night. I stirred my fires and the eyes disappeared for a time, but they returned. Maybe whatever was in the darkness was waiting for me to get fresh firewood, I don't know. But as I burned up my supply of firewood and my fires grew low, the eyes came closer.

I yelled and threw rocks at the animal, but it did little good. I knew it wasn't a coyote, because I recalled Papa saying that coyotes seldom come remotely close to fire; but that was of little consolation to me.

I looked for other eyes in the darkness, but there was only one pair. I touched my tongue to my dry lips, wishing for a drink of water, but had none. It seemed like I didn't have anything: no gun, no water, no food, no blanket. I sank to my knees, pleading with the Lord. "I don't mind dying, God, but I don't want to be eaten by a bear, or whatever is out there." I wondered if it would hurt to be eaten by a big animal. Would it kill me before it started eating me?

My fires were down to coals, and the animal drew nearer. It must be hungry. I took a deep breath, blew it out slowly the way Papa had taught me when shooting his flintlock gun, and held my knife in readiness.

Hugging the earth, the animal approached. At last I got a half decent look at my enemy, looking death in the mouth. Muscular and tawny, it wasn't a wolf or a bear, but looked somewhat like a large house cat, stalking a mouse. I was the mouse, and not happy with my lot.

With deadly caution the big cat closed in, not quite sure if it was ready to brave the remains of my fires, but not noticeably afraid,

either. I forced myself to be calm, 'cause my life depended on it.

The cat opened its mouth in a throaty hiss, like a house cat fighting a dog. It was my one chance. With all my might I threw my knife into the part of the animal that captured my attention, the black hole of his mouth. The throw was true, but what good is a knife down an animal's throat?

The animal seemed to turn inside out, snarling and biting, trying to spit out the knife. It flung itself on the ground, and suddenly I saw a red willow in its side. On the end of the willow were feathers . . . guide feathers, which made it look like the end of an arrow.

It *was* an arrow!

The thrashing subsided. A few more twitches, and the animal lay still. My mouth dry and my heart in my throat, I held my second knife in readiness, peering into the darkness. Whoever had shot the arrow, probably an Indian, would soon make his appearance.

I waited. Time passed and my knees were getting weak.

Like a shadow in the night, the Indian appeared. With all my strength I threw my knife, because I surely wasn't about to have my arms and legs lopped off by a heathen Lamanite. I heard the thud as the knife struck, then felt a blow to my head as something, thrown by the Indian, struck me almighty hard. All went black.

It was full light when I awoke. I looked around, wondering, and my eyes settled on an Indian squatting on his haunches across the fire from me. Meat was roasting on a spit above the low frame. While studying me with hard eyes, the Indian sliced off a sliver of hot meat, stuffed it in his mouth and chewed it contentedly.

The meat was probably from whatever I . . . we . . . had killed, and looked and smelled good. I started to move, but my hands seemed awkward. I looked down and saw that they were tied with a braided leather rope.

The Indian was dressed in a type of coat with the hair turned in; I guessed it was made from a buffalo hide. I thought I saw a small bloody slit in his coat, near his heart, 'bout where I had aimed the knife when I threw it at him the previous night. His leggings, too, had the hair turned in, as did his moccasins. On his head was a coyote hat, the coyote's beady eyes as cold as the Indian's. I looked at him through pleading eyes and said, "Food." He paid me no mind, but continued his eating.

Hearing movement, I looked over my shoulder and saw a calico horse munching grass. Apparently the Indian had uncovered the grass, as most of the grass was covered with snow.

My hands were tied in front of me, and I saw that I could easily untie the rope with my teeth. So while the Indian watched, I busied myself untying my hands. One of my knives lay on a rock near the fire. When I had untied my hands, I eased myself toward the rock and grabbed the knife. Saying nothing, the Indian watched me. He was still watching as I slid up to the fire across from him and sliced off some meat. I noticed my stomach was growling, but paid it no mind.

He watched me and I watched him as we both chewed the juicy meat. It wasn't the most tender meat I'd ever eaten, but it was good. I had to eat slowly because my stomach seemed to be stretching with every swallow.

For a long time we both ate, chewing slowly and thoroughly. I wiped off my knife and put it in its sheath, then looked around for my second knife. It was only a short distance from the first, and I slid it into its sheath. All this time the Indian was eating slowly, and I marveled at the quantity of food he was consuming.

Rising, I made my way to the river and drank deeply from its gray water. Then I returned to the fire. It was clear that the Indian wasn't going to speak until he was good and ready. But to my surprise, when he finished eating, he saddled his horse with a crude Indian saddle, leaped onto it in one easy bound, and nudged the horse.

"Wait," I yelled, running after him, catching his rope stirrup. It brought him up short, and he looked at me through hard, solitary black eyes. I let go, wondering what I was doing. I had thrown my knife at him; but after all, I was just a ten-year-old who looked like eight. He booted his horse and disappeared through the trees, leaving me standing there flat-footed, alone again.

SHUNKTOKECHA

F OR LONG MOMENTS I watched the spot where I had last seen the Indian. More alone than I had ever been, I'd thrown a knife at the only human I had seen.

I glanced at the river, gray under the winter sky. Fog concealed the opposite bank, possibly a quarter of a mile across the river's angry surface. The trees around me were as bare as skeletons, the breeze gently whispering through the naked branches. "Mama," I whispered, "why did you have to leave me? Why did you and Papa go to Jesus without me?" I pulled my coat tighter around me; it wasn't nearly warm enough.

A growing anger was gnawing inside me—an anger against the Missourians with blackened faces who had driven us out of our home, shot Papa, and left Mama and Papa to die. Just thinking about it, my mind flashed back to Papa's red eyes as he said, "She's gone to live with Jesus." I shook it off because Papa said that when you're angry you can't think straight. Besides, in a few days I might be standing before Jesus in heaven, where the streets are paved with gold, whatever that was worth. The only gold I had ever seen was a tiny twenty-dollar gold coin, which wasn't particularly impressive.

Down the river, who knows how far, was New Orleans, though I would have to slip past Independence to reach it. Could I walk it? Was it fifty miles? . . . a hundred? . . . two hundred? Someone had said it was a thousand miles, but a thousand miles was probably all the way around the world. A thousand was just a big word that meant it was farther than you wanted to count, like when your mother sent you into the cabin to wash about a thousand dishes, or when Papa gave you about a thousand rows of corn to hoe.

Glancing at my fire, my eyes rested on the remains of the meat, curing in the smoke. The Indian had taken some meat with him, but there was still a lot left. I wouldn't be hungry for a few days, but I might want to move farther from the river. It is humid and cold on the banks of a river in winter, they say.

I cut my meat into smaller chunks so that it would cure faster, wishing I knew how to tell when the meat was cured. Papa took his hams to Brother Archibald's smokehouse to cure, and in a week or so he brought them back home, but I didn't know what that meant. Were they being cured all that time?

I had it in mind to hike along the shoreline, hoping to find my boat washed ashore downstream, but did I dare leave my meat to smoke while I was away? My fires had saved me from the big cat, but still he had approached, waiting his chance to get me. I had kept the fire going 'til I ran out of wood, but it's a lot easier to keep a cooking fire going than a smoking fire. For one thing, the breeze wants to blow the smoke out from under the meat, or the fire dies out for want of flame, leaving the meat available to be snatched by any predator that comes along.

I decided to take my chances and make a short expedition, but first I made a walking stick. Walking sticks aren't for walking, they're for striking anything on the head that wants to make you their dinner, or for pushing reeds aside to see what's in a thicket before you plunge in.

Two hours later and a half mile down the river, I found a creek that fed into the Missouri from the west, though I didn't see anything of the little rowboat. If I followed the creek, I reasoned, I wouldn't get lost, and it would lead me away from the cold river.

So the next morning I said goodbye to the Missouri and headed west along the creek, carrying my meat in a crude reed basket.

The snow was no longer crunchy and my feet were always wet, as my shoes were in sore need of fat to waterproof 'em. Still, I shuffled along, looking for I didn't know what. The only thing I found that was edible was cattails. Eating cattails, even when roasted, is about like eating cotton. But it does fill your stomach, and when eaten with smoked meat, isn't too bad.

When night came, I wished for the river bank to reflect my fire, but had to make my own reflector. I made two reflectors at angles to each other, laid small stuff across the top, and that night slept warmer than I'd slept since the mobbing.

That night I dreamed the Indian returned, tomahawk in hand, to lop off my arms and legs. When I woke from the nightmare in a sweat, there he was, hunkered down across the fire from me, cold eyes calculating how he was a-goin' to begin his satanic torture. I reached for my knife, but it wasn't there. The savage had me dead to rights.

I've never been too good at taking pain, but I'm no baby, either. Any boy who has lived among the godless Missouri gentile boys for a few years, as I had done, learns a bit about how to survive. So I set my jaw and looked the savage straight in his cold, black eyes, waiting for him to be the first to speak, if indeed he knew how to talk.

"Shunktokecha," he said, pointing to himself. Surprised, I guessed he was trying to tell me his name. "Shunktokecha," he repeated, again pointing to himself. It was the kind of name that my tongue didn't want to tangle with. In time I learned it meant "coyote" or "wolf." A third time the Indian repeated his name, and I responded with "Shunk," which was good enough for him.

"Sam," I said, pointing to myself. He repeated it. His face was dark, and his eyes black. What I had taken for cold black eyes were just black, maybe even a little warm black. As we talked, he was teaching me Pawnee and Sioux words, and that's all he did for days: fire, tree, hot, cold, wind, buffalo, deer, knife, tomahawk.

Shunk didn't ask me to go with him. When he was ready to leave, he just gave me his hand, and I swung up behind him. I learned later that no one sits in front of a warrior on a horse, 'cept maybe a little child. The warrior needs his hands free. When you're riding behind a warrior, he doesn't wear his bow over his shoulder, he carries his bow in one hand. He could use two hands if he wanted, because usually Indians guide their mounts with their knees, even when straddling one of their Indian saddles. Their mounts are well trained, reared on love, and often the warrior's only companion. They have to be well trained, because with the Indian's poor excuse of a saddle, you can't remain astride the pony for long unless the pony wants you there. Indian ponies are as affectionate as dogs.

As we traveled, I learned much about Shunk and myself. I learned that in the Indian world, names have to be earned, then pronounced upon you by a medicine man. Sometimes your name changes as you perform different noted deeds. They're names such as "Bit a Bear," "Antler Arm," or "Snake Eyes," and they all come with a story of how the warrior earned his name. My name was always "Knife Thrower," and the story of my throwing a knife at Shunk was ofttimes repeated. Apparently the point of the knife penetrated his buffalo coat and was only stopped by a rib bone. I shudder to think what life would have been like had I actually killed him.

But Shunk was not your usual Pawnee. It was whispered that he was a coward, as he refused to go on raiding parties except to hold the horses. He had never counted coup on a raiding party, so no maiden would have him as her husband.

In Pawnee custom, "counting coup" refers to the ceremonial touching of an enemy warrior. Most often the enemy is killed and the scalp taken for evidence, as an enemy's life has little value in the Pawnee culture. Counting coup can be done without killing if there is a witness, but generally the enemy loses his life.

Shunk wasn't really Pawnee; he was Sioux, captured as a twelve-year-old half-grown boy and adopted by a poor Pawnee family that needed his services to hunt meat. He was one of the better hunters in the village, maybe the best . . . I don't know.

THE
PAWNEE VILLAGE

I CAN'T SAY THAT I LIKED SHUNK, at least not at first. But he was a human being, someone for company. I hadn't even classified the Missouri mobsters as human beings. After doing what they had done to Mama and Papa, I called them just animals, nothing more.

We didn't seem as we were going anywhere—just wandering, as far as I could tell. I didn't always ride, either; I trotted alongside 'til I thought I would die, then I trotted some more. I had to take off my shoes, because as far as I was concerned shoes were only for keeping your feet warm while walking in the snow, or for going to church. For running, even in light snow, shoes are useless.

Shunk and I had been together for nearly two weeks when we struck a western course to his Pawnee village, several days' ride northwest and a day's ride into prairie grass country. Soon we passed the first sentries to the village, and I knew something was wrong because Shunk grew tense. In the distance I could hear the most hideous wailing you ever heard. Shunk stopped and tied a cord around my neck, then had me trot beside his Calico horse like a dog on a leash. I was plumb humiliated, but he didn't give me any explanation. Later, I learned it was a way of telling the whole village to leave me alone, because I was his property.

In two inches of slushy snow I trotted into the village, and would just as leave have turned right around and skedaddled out of there. Men and women alike had black soot on their faces, and the women were wailing the death chant, though at the time I didn't know what it was. Some women had blood freely flowing from their arms and faces, and their expressions were distorted in agony. I later learned that in the autumn a group of feisty young warriors had gone to count coup, because they had to have counted coup to be eligible to propose marriage. (When they're of a certain age, warriors seem blinded by marriage.) But the group had not chosen a weak village to count coup on, and the lone survivor had just made it home, wounded and on foot, with his gruesome report.

It was a poor time for Shunk to introduce me, because he was far from a big man in the tribe. As he led me like a dog on a leash, the tribe's anger seemed directed toward both Shunk and me, and I faltered. Yet he couldn't back out, because we had already been seen by the village sentries.

Shunk stopped his pony in front of a shaggy-looking lodge and jumped off, tying the calico loosely to a post that was taller than a man's head. Indians don't swing off their ponies as do white men, because their saddles aren't secured to their mounts well enough to support their weight on one rope stirrup. They slip their left leg in front of them and jump off to the right. They always mount from the right side, too.

As he turned after securing his mount, Shunk was accosted by a wailing woman with a blackened face. I knew what she was calling him, because he had taught me, thinking it better that he tell me than let me find out from someone else. She was calling him a coward.

Beating on Shunk's chest with her doubled fists, the woman repeatedly taunted, "Coward, coward, coward!" I have to admit that none of Shunk's actions indicated anything but a coward, standing there stone-still while a black-faced imp beat on his chest. But what did I know?

The woman then grabbed a stone knife from the belt of a bystander and came at me, blood dripping off her chin from a gash on her left cheek. Whether she really intended to use the knife on me, I surely didn't know and wasn't about to find out. I'd looked into the devilish faces of Missouri mobsters with blackened faces, and this Pawnee woman with soot on her face didn't look much different.

My hand sought my throwing knife at the nape of my neck. As if in a trance, I was no longer looking into a woman's face, but into the face of the mobster who had shot Papa. My fingers closed on my knife and my body relaxed. In an instant the mobster would die!

"Stop!" The words rang out like the bellowing of a bull, and the whole camp froze. Like a majestic warrior, Shunk stood there, in command. The woman slunk to the sidelines like a whipped puppy. He ripped open his shirt and, pointing to his heart, ordered, "Throw!" Even in my limited Pawnee, I knew the command, because my name was Knife Thrower. The bystanders looked on in deathly silence. Possibly this was the first time Shunk had issued such an order.

"Throw," he said again, but this time he was almost pleading. In that instant I knew that Shunk was sick of life and wanted to go live with Jesus. Bishop Whitney would have said I had a testimony that Shunk wanted to die. Shunk made a sign that he wanted the blade to enter at an angle so that it would slip through his ribs to his heart.

A pony snorted, and from out in the prairie a mourner wailed. My knife was halfway out of its sheath, and I had set every muscle for a throw hard enough to sink the blade deep into the mobster's heart. Yet in spite of Shunk's faith in me, I had not practiced throwing a knife at an angle so that it would slip between a man's ribs, and this was not the time to practice.

With all my might I threw the best throw I had ever made, and heard the solid thud as the knife buried itself deep into the post by Shunk's head. It penetrated the cape of his coyote cap, pinning it solidly to the post. He looked disappointed, and maybe he was. Then he slipped his head out from under his cap and left it pinned to the post.

Someone at my left used the word for coward, but directed it at me. It seemed he was calling me a coward because I didn't kill Shunk. As I learned later, he should have thought better of his remarks, as his family relied on Shunk for meat. Shunk provided much meat for several families.

My accuser was a boy who appeared to be a couple of years older than me and doubtless thought I was younger than I was. But we paleface boys are tough as nails, 'cuz most of us are out at the wood yard chopping firewood as soon as we shed our diapers. Pawnee boys can beat white boys every time in agility and running, but as far as solid arm and shoulder muscles are concerned, they can't beat us woodchoppers. I slid my hand in my pocket and wrapped my fingers around Papa's little hunk of steel that he used to strike fires.

As my hand came out, the boy taunted me a second time by calling me a coward. He had just gotten the words out of his mouth when my fist sank into the pit of his stomach with all the force my woodchopping muscles could muster. I drove my fist clean to his backbone with enough force to lift him to his toes. As he bent over trying to get his wind, my second blow caught him on the back of his shoulder, driving him to the snow. It was the type of mercy the gentile Missouri boys had shown me. None.

Knocked to the ground, his face was in slush. I was afraid he would drown, so I quickly rolled him over and wiped the slush from his mouth. That act caused other boys to again call me a coward. Seems I was in one of those "damned if you do, damned if you don't" situations. But my effort to keep the boy from drowning was not lost on the boy's sister, White Rabbit, who, in years to come, would mean as much to me as life itself.

Like a revelation, it dawned on the crowd that a captive boy had just flattened a villager. Before I could straighten up, villagers were all over me, hitting, poking, shoving, biting. The woman with the knife pushed through the crowd. I saw her hideous blackened, bloody face as she raised the knife.

"Stop!" Shunk yelled, and rattled off a sentence in Pawnee that I wasn't near capable of understanding. An arrow was fit to his drawn bow, and his lips quivered in anticipation. It wasn't that Shunk had much of a right to interfere, because he didn't, as he had never counted coup. Still, much of the village's poor depended on his hunting skills for food, and in the Moon of Difficulty (January), Indians liked to stay on the good side of their better hunters. Besides, the woman had violated a tribal law: she had attempted to kill a guest. Anyone who visits a village, or is brought in, is safe as long as he remains in the village. The exception is a captive, like myself, but only the owner of the captive can allow him to be killed or tortured. The leash around my neck told everyone that Shunk was my owner.

Some people don't think that Indians have law and order, but they do. They also have a police force. The village police surrounded me, and the old men put their heads together. It was clear that a law had been broken, but the actions of the woman could be excused, as she was in mourning.

"Take your property and hide him in your lodge during the period of mourning," an old man said. "He is yours, and you will be his uncle." It was more than just saying that I could live. The old men were recognizing that I had shown bravery, thus earning the right to be a person, and Shunk was ordered to be my uncle (teacher). In the Indian matriarchal society, a woman can usually pick either her husband or her brother as a trainer for her son, depending on what other duties the man has been assigned by the tribe.

An old man put his hand to my throwing knife to pull it out, but couldn't extract it. It made me wonder, as at the time I hadn't realized that the Pawnee, being accustomed to stone knives, didn't dare pull on a knife hard, for fear it would break. They had never seen a knife thrown, as you don't throw stone knives. A wave of murmurs went through the crowd, so a second warrior tried, but didn't pull out the blade.

I stepped right up and noticed that the knife had struck a vertical split in the post and had sunk two inches into the crack. The knife was as high as I could reach, so I had to stretch. I put my foot on the post, with both hands on the knife, and pulled as hard as I could, but the knife was stuck in the crack. With renewed vigor I again pulled. The blade finally broke loose, and I fell onto my back in the snow as the Indians roared with laughter. I soon found that Indians have a humorous streak and love to laugh at themselves and each other.

HOME
SWEET HOME

AN OLD LADY STEPPED UP and took my leash. Her name was Herb Woman, a medicine woman and Shunk's adoptive mother, though I wasn't told that at the time. To me she was just an old lady with a face as hard as nails. She lifted my leash from where it lay in the slush and handed it to an older girl who, I soon learned, had seen fourteen winters. The girl yanked my leash so hard that the crowd started laughing, but I surely didn't. She was showing me who was boss, and for the next two weeks she made my life so unbearable that I wished I was back with the Missouri boys. I had always been happy that I didn't have a bossy older sister, but that was about to change.

I was taken into the lodge, a buffalo hide tepee, and they told me the family rules as best they could. The girl's name was Pick-a-Coal, and she took great pains in making sure I pronounced it correctly. There was also a younger girl in my new family who had seen eight winters and seven summers. She went by the name of Little Star, which was a child's name, but she liked it and never did ask for an adult name. Of course, I eventually learned that children don't have to ask for new names; they are sometimes revealed to the tribe by Ti-rá-wa (The Great Spirit). Then the candidate washes and purifies himself or herself, either in a sweat lodge or in the smoke of a ceremonial fire, dresses in fresh skins, and is ceremonially given his or her new name by the medicine man.

The girl's father had died in a coup raid when Shunk had seen fourteen summers. From then on Shunk became the family's only hunter of meat. He also provided meat for families of dead warriors who the tribe said had been more valiant than he, meaning that they had gone off counting coup and had been honorably killed.

The girls called Herb Woman "Grandmother," so I, thinking that was her name, called her Grandmother, too. Unwittingly I had done the right thing, as in Indian families the adults are always referred to by their title, which is why I called Shunk "Uncle."

In Pawnee families, child discipline is nearly unheard of. Children can get away with almost anything, which was particularly hard for me, a captive. No matter what they did to me, nobody stopped them. Of course, that is how Pick-a-Coal got her name. If babies want to crawl into the fire or pick up a coal, they're allowed to, but they usually only do it once. Pick-a-Coal had to do it twice to learn, so was awarded the name. Indian parents don't have to constantly yell at their children to stay out of the fire, as do paleface parents.

Being bossy seemed to come natural to Pick-a-Coal, and her rules didn't make sense. For example, at night she made me sleep without a buffalo robe covering me, and neither Grandmother nor Shunk interfered, as it was the children's right to treat a captive any way they liked.

As winter advanced into spring, buffalo chips became scarce. What buffalo chips there were had to be saved for cooking, so our lodge was cold. At night the fire was allowed to die out, the smoke flaps closed, and I was left to lie on the floor shivering. Except for the fire ring, the tepee was carpeted with raw buffalo robes, so the floor was soft. I used my coat as a quilt, but it wasn't nearly warm enough without a fire.

On one cold night I felt a hand on my arm, and saw it was Grandmother, gently drawing me to her. She pulled me under her buffalo robe with her. I basked in the warmth of her body, and it seemed like Mama was there when she wrapped her arms around me and we fell asleep together.

The next night again there was no fire, and Grandmother did not invite me to share her robes. Again I lay shivering. This time I felt Pick-a-Coal's hand on my arm, drawing me to her. I didn't object because I was cold, but I didn't like sleeping with her and Little Star because they were girls. Still, I slid in where it was warm and went to sleep.

Gradually I learned that in Indian families, children sleep as a family under the same robe until their later years, when they feel too mature to sleep with the kids. In my ignorance of Indian ways, I was showing an affront to the family by not sliding into the children's bed and going to sleep. From then on I was treated better by Pick-a-Coal and Little Star, who figured I had finally decided to stop snubbing them. Actually, Pick-a-Coal was old enough to have a bed of her own, but hadn't made the move. Again, using Indian logic, it was her decision because she was old enough to think for herself.

Meals in the lodge were available twice a day: early morning and late evening. We had a lot of meat and wild rice; also beans that were pirated from mice and muskrat nests. The girls dug teepsinna (wild turnips) and wild sweet potatoes, and Grandmother had herbs for everything. Meat was roasted, cooked in the stomachs of animals, or baked in a steam pit. Though sometimes we cut meat directly from a roast as we ate it, Grandmother also had wooden bowls we could use. When we boys were too far away from the lodge to make it home, we would roast a small animal, or cook a fish or bird in the white ashes under the fire. Fish, caught with wild hemp or horsehair lines, were just buried in the ashes, but birds were dipped in water before they were buried in the ashes. After cooking the birds in their own juices, the skin and feathers easily came off together and you picked off the meat as you ate, leaving the skeleton of the bird intact.

As religiously as my Mormon family, grace was said before

each meal, though the words didn't vary. Grandmother's grace prayer was, "Great Mystery, do thou partake of this venison (or whatever we had), and still be gracious!" It may seem like a strange grace, but it made perfect sense to us.

Every evening, Little Star and I gave an accounting of ourselves to either Grandmother or Uncle. At first it was distasteful to me, as they wanted us to rehearse in detail all the birds, animals, and plants we had seen. Animals were divided into four classes: those that walk on four legs, those that creep, those that swim with fins, and those that fly. Birds were usually divided by color or size . . . any way we wanted to divide them . . . and Grandmother, Uncle, or Pick-a-Coal provided the names. After a few weeks the nightly drills were no longer distasteful, and I actually looked forward to them. No matter what I saw, someone cared and wanted, even demanded, a detailed report.

INDIAN TO THE CORE

MY SKIN BECAME LAMANITE the first summer...so tanned and full of paint that it was nearly permanently tattooed. My hair, too, was so full of paint that it lacked color of its own, making me no longer a "paleface" but a "white-eyes," short for "white man's eyes," as my pale eyes are green. My mind, too, became Lamanite; and as I reflected on my boyhood memories of the white man's magic, I wondered how much was real and how much was a child's fantasy.

I remembered the boat that walked on water (steam boat), the boat that walked on mountains (locomotive), the powdered coal that exploded (gun powder), and the eye that made your vision leap (telescope). But most of all I remembered the blackened faces of the Missouri mobsters, and I wondered if their faces were really as hideous as my memory told me, or if my childhood imagination had made them bigger than life.

Still, I recalled going to a Missouri village with Papa and Mama, where a wealthy man had called a big feast and made much food. Everyone from off the street was invited, and they came and ate their fill. But when they were leaving after the feast, the wealthy man demanded payment for the food eaten. You couldn't even take a parsnip from a paleface's garden without paying, as I recalled, which made me wonder about white men's ways.

I remembered the Bible and the Book of Mormon with fondness, repeatedly telling the stories to my Pawnee family. "When you become a warrior, will you take me to find the book? Will you read it to me?" Uncle asked.

"We will find it," I said, "but I don't know if I still remember how to read. Yet finding it is very dangerous because the Missourians say, 'The only good Indian is a dead Indian.' To travel their hunting grounds, we would have to steal white men's clothes and put white clay on our faces so that they would be pale."

It was my thirteenth summer, and I was no longer small for my age. I stood head and shoulders above the other boys, and I was still growing.

My best friend was Gray Owl, the lad I had decked when I first entered the village. Gray Owl's sister, White Rabbit, was my first love, though I surely wouldn't have admitted it to anyone alive, especially to Gray Owl, as I would have been teased unmercifully.

The Pawnee teased each other, and all took it in stride, as it was considered rude to take offense when you were being teased. Villagers collected in the council lodge to swap stories as they sat with their knees against their chests, held in place by their buffalo robes, creating an Indian version of a rocking chair. Some stories were serious and some spiritual, but most were humorous. You laughed so hard that your side ached, and some storytellers wore comical masks to make the stories merrier. No villager was immune from the onslaught of tribal humor, so I was almighty careful not to let my feelings for White Rabbit known, lest she be embarrassed.

One day Gray Owl's little brother, Fleet-of-Foot, wanted to go with us larger boys as we made war on a nest of hornets. It wasn't that I liked him around, though I didn't mind much, because White Rabbit was his sister.

Our plan was to count coup on a nest of hornets, pretending they were Crow warriors. Indian boys usually only play games that resemble what they will do as adults.

We started our war on the hornets with a scalp dance, whooping it up and slashing the air with our tomahawks. Our mock dance resembled the real thing, complete with war paint that colored our brown bodies. Fleet-of-Foot joined in with all the energy his eight summers could muster. White Rabbit watched from the sidelines, which made it even better.

Two miles from the village was a rather large stream, and on its northern bank was the hornet's nest, making it a two-mile run from the village. Pretending it was a Crow village, we crept close, making our every movement blend with the wave of the grass. On a given signal we whooped the Pawnee war cry and descended on the Crow village, smashing their home and counting coup.

Fleet-of-Foot was only fleet when compared to boys his age, but he didn't want to be outdone. He threw himself on the smashed nest and declared with dignity, "I, Fleet-of-Foot, mighty Pawnee warrior, count coup on the hideous Crow. Gray Owl is my witness!" Suddenly Fleet-of-Foot started screaming, and an older boy yelled, "Jump into the water! Jump into the water!" Fleet-of-Foot obeyed, stumbling once. Some older boys also took to the water, though many pretend Crow scalps were taken.

We packed Fleet-of-Foot's stings in mud, and gave him some inner bark of the red willow to chew. But that evening at our victory dance he was ignored, as if he didn't exist. He wasn't allowed to dance with the rest, as the hornets had counted coup on him. What's worse, he sat with a long face because he had screamed, and that flaw was likely to show itself at other times in his life. White Rabbit was at the dance, and I noticed her studying her little brother. Yet even in his misery she didn't go to him, as that would have been inappropriate.

White Rabbit was like that: concerned for the feelings of others. But she nearly broke my heart when in my fourteenth spring she studied my facial hairs and wrinkled up her nose. Pawnee boys pull out what few facial hairs they have, but I had far too many to pull out.

I recalled seeing Papa scrape his lathered face with a razor. I didn't have any lather, but I had two nice throwing knives. I retired to the creek and painstakingly honed my knife, trying to make a razor out of it. I didn't have a mirror, hadn't even seen one since the mob drove us from our Missouri home. But I shaved as best I could.

Proud of my careful grooming, I made it a point to pass White Rabbit's lodge as I entered the village. White Rabbit just stared, and I stopped, hoping she was pleased. Gently she touched my face and her fingers came away bloody.

"I just shaved," I explained.

"Oh?" she replied. "Did you use a tomahawk?"

I excused myself and sought out a quiet pool to examine my reflection. Even before I got to the pool I noticed that blood had started dripping from my chin. Indians, who don't have as much taboo over body functions as do whites, urinate on small cuts . . . it keeps down infections. But that sounded impractical, seeing as how the cuts were on my face. Papa used drinking alcohol on his face after he saved. After he applied the alcohol to his skin he always took a swallow, saying it was good for the blood.

I desperately wanted to talk with Papa . . . to ask him how white people shaved. Of course that was out, so the next day when Uncle returned from a hunt, I approached the subject.

"Do you know how paleface men shave?" I asked.

"No," he replied. "The paleface who visited me didn't have hair on his face."

"What paleface?" I asked.

Suddenly Uncle looked as if he had let something slip that he had been trying to keep hidden. He glanced at Grandmother, who was busy preparing the antelope he had just brought. "I will speak of it later," he replied, and wandered down to the creek to wash the antelope blood from his garments.

That evening I found Uncle alone, straightening arrows. "Tell me about the paleface man who didn't have to shave," I said.

"He . . . he was one of the three men you told about, Knife Thrower."

"What three?"

"The three whose story is written in the book you read as a paleface child. You have told us the story often."

"The Three Nephites?"

"Ho (yes)."

"You mean you've seen them?"

"I have only seen one . . . many Indians have seen him."

"Why didn't you tell me?"

"It is very sacred . . . and very personal."

"When did you see him?"

"I saw him in my sixteenth summer."

"Wha . . . what did he say?"

"He said, 'Do not count coup.'"

"But Uncle, if you do not count coup, no woman will have you, and you will always live alone. Even now you have seen twenty-five summers, when most warriors get married at twenty-two or twenty-three summers."

"I do not wish to displease the Great Mystery," he replied with a shrug.

MAIDEN FEAST

A WARRIOR NAMED TONKA seemed impressed with Pick-a-Coal, but she wasn't impressed with him, and worried for fear Tonka was the suitor who had been meeting her on the path to the creek. To palefaces, it seems odd that a girl would not know her suitor, but not so in the Indian world.

The men of our village put their buffalo robes over their heads when courting, then they position themselves on the paths the maidens have to use in getting water or firewood. Maybe a suitor will tell a maiden of her grace or beauty, who knows? What do boys tell girls when courting?

We were camped on the edge of the forest, with the chattering noises of the animal tribes so loud it made your head swim. On the prairie it's incredibly quiet, a sharp contrast to the forest.

Hunting was good, which gave the warriors a lot of free time to spend courting, and the girls didn't seem to mind. I would have liked to be a courter, but I had only seen fifteen springs. So I watched the proceedings, sometimes envying, sometimes disgusted. But Pick-a-Coal had seen nineteen springs, which made her old enough to marry.

She came into the lodge one evening and didn't seem to have her mind on anything, 'cept maybe the wind whistling across the smoke flap. She ate her meal in silence, hardly letting us draw her into any family conversation, so we knew her interest was elsewhere.

We had just completed the evening meal, when out of the darkness came the chattering of a squirrel. It didn't take any brains to know it wasn't a real squirrel, as there were many tepees between us and the nearest tree. Besides, it was dark and the squirrels were probably in their lodges holding hands, or whatever courting squirrels do.

Pick-a-Coal tensed, then started stirring the fire. It looked like she was trying to rub the fire out, and it started smoking. "I'll adjust the smoke flaps," she said, and swished through the lodge entrance. How obvious, I thought.

We heard her working with the smoke flap poles, adjusting and readjusting them. We all looked at each other, as a family does. It was Pick-a-Coal's show . . . we were just along for the ride.

We could hear the sounds of the night, but were straining for squirrel sounds . . . sounds from the two-legged squirrel tribe. Minutes later Pick-a-Coal was stomping back to the tepee as delicately as a buffalo. She flung open the thick buffalo hump that did duty for a door, and stepped in, her face clouded in disgust. She threw herself to the buffalo carpet, drew her knees to her chest, wrapped her buffalo robe around her, and started rocking, maybe a bit faster than normal. No one spoke. Fact is, we barely breathed.

Suddenly Uncle uttered a beautiful rendition of a squirrel's chatter. Pick-a-Coal allowed a whisk of a grin to cross her face and spit out her explanation in one word, "Tonka," as if he were something loath.

I suppose Tonka was handsome enough, though I'm surely not a judge of that. But the maidens' gossip circuit had it on good authority that he had taken advantage of maidens. He was old enough to marry and had counted coup, but his success in battle was not lost in his well-developed ego, something village girls noticed. Nothing more was said about Tonka, as there are some things you tease big sisters about, and some things you leave alone.

The following week, the village crier rode through our village announcing the multi-village Maiden Feast, to take place at Rice Lake, a local lake noted for the wild rice swamps on its sunset shores. It could almost be called "Courting Lake," because during wild rice season couples meet on the canoe trails through the swamp. During the early days of the harvest when the maidens are tying the rice into bundles, the warriors learn their favorite maiden's assigned area. Then, when the maiden returns in a few days to knock the heads of rice into the bottom of her canoe or buffalo boat, she finds a suitor waiting for her, willing to share her work load.

The Maiden Feast, to take place on Rice Lake's swamp-free sunrise shores, was only for pure maidens. The maidens not only had to declare themselves pure, but the unmarried warriors and older boys were on hand to speak up if an impure maiden attempted to join the feast. It also provided an opportunity for the warriors to look over eligible maidens from other villages.

A large rock, painted red, was used as an altar. Beside it, two arrows were loosely stuck into the ground. In declaring herself pure, the maiden gently brushes their feathers, careful not to dislodge the arrows, then touches the huge red rock, accompanied by jokes from the warriors advising her not to knock over the rock. Then, if no warrior or older boy challenges her, she enters the pure maiden's circle. Behind the circle, the older women and chaperones proudly keep watch.

I watched White Rabbit enter the circle, and there was a lump in my throat as I realized she would likely be long married before I became eligible to court her. As I glanced at the eligible warriors, they seemed to be licking their chops like wolves after a fawn. My eyes rested on Tonka as he studied Pick-a-Coal, who had not yet declared herself. Suddenly it occurred to me that Tonka was vindictive and about to cause trouble.

Overhead a hawk soared, effortlessly riding the breeze. Maybe it was an omen from the bird tribe that watches all . . . I don't know.

The next two maidens declared themselves, then it was Pick-a-Coal's turn. Straight and tall in a white doeskin dress ornamented with porcupine quills, she stepped forward, lightly brushed the arrow feathers, then touched the rock. But as she made her way to the maiden's circle, Tonka spoke up.

"I'm sorry," he proudly said, "but according to the customs of our people, you shouldn't be here. Seven days ago you went with me to the trees." His face was hard, yet I suspected that inside he was smirking. Blinded by his own importance as a scalp-carrying warrior, it didn't seem to me that he was thinking straight. 'Course I never did give Tonka much credit for brains, and was surprised when he had returned home from the raid with Sioux scalps, much less his own scalp intact.

Pick-a-Coal was caught off guard; at least that was how it appeared to me. Yet she recovered quickly and stood there straight and tall, poised like a goddess. Right then and there I knew Tonka was in trouble, as I'd been her brother long enough to know that the likes of Tonka didn't stand a prayer against her quick tongue.

"It is true that Tonka courted me seven days ago," she said, "and he invited me to the trees with him, but I did not accept. He did such a poor imitation of a squirrel that the whole lodge knew I was called out. Therefore Grandmother and Uncle are my witnesses that I wasn't with Tonka long enough to go any-where, much less to the trees."

For long moments not a word was spoken. A bee buzzed, but all humans held their breath. Then someone snickered, and everyone laughed. Indians will laugh at anything funny, and the mental picture of a maiden rebuffing a puffed-up warrior was well painted. As I said, I never did give Tonka too much credit for brains.

The old men could have called on Uncle for a testimony, but then they would have been pitting a hunter's testimony against the testimony of a warrior. Even the old men figured hunters were beneath warriors, yet they were almighty respectful of the hunters, because when a warrior is killed the hunters are depended upon to feed the warrior's widow and children. It requires different skills to be a warrior than a hunter, as warriors value quick off-hand shooting, while hunters go for long-range accuracy. So most warriors depend on buffalo for their meat, because to kill buffalo you ride in close and shoot into the side of the animal, aiming for the heart.

Still, the testimony of a maiden has equal weight with the testimony of a warrior in courting affairs, so the crowd looked to the matriarchs, who nodded in favor of Pick-a-Coal. After all, the matriarchs had heard the same gossip about Tonka's moral character as had the maidens, and knew that few maidens would take the chance of being seen with him.

The old men nodded to the police, who led Tonka away. I didn't know what chastisement he would receive, as it's a serious offense to discredit a maiden. But as he passed Pick-a-Coal he cast her a long, hard look, and I had the feeling we hadn't heard the last of Tonka's vindictiveness.

TONKA'S REVENGE

IT TOOK A MOON for Tonka to find a way to strike in revenge, but when he struck, it hurt deeply.

Uncle and I had been hunting together, as I was old enough to do my share as a hunter. Trained in long-range accuracy by Uncle, when I needed quick, off-hand shooting I usually used my throwing knife. Uncle only carried long-range arrows with him, made with long-grain wood that he purchased from wandering traders, and arrowheads expertly fashioned by the best arrowhead chippers.

We were hunting antelope but ran across two buffaloes, a cow and a huge calf. I prefer buffalo meat to antelope meat, and so does most everyone else. We bellied in close, and at Uncle's signal we both let our arrows fly. 'Course the arrows flew true, as there was nothing wrong with our marksmanship or our arrows.

Two buffaloes were about as much meat as we wanted to drag back to the village; but as we approached our kill, we saw that we were on the edge of a buffalo wallow that contained a dozen lazy creatures. So we took to our bellies again and studied the situation.

Most of the buffaloes were old mossy horn bulls, too tough for anything but coyotes or wolves. We made careful note of the young buffaloes in the wallow, then each chose our targets and laid out several arrows. My initial target was a blunt horn, and second I would try for a six-toother (six-year-old cow). I let my first arrow fly slightly after Uncle's, then in rapid succession we killed as many creatures as we could. In all we killed nine buffaloes, and those that got away were too old to be worth much.

It was far too much meat for two hunters to drag back to the village alone, so Uncle assigned me to ride to the village and get help. We had in mind to have the needy families ride to the kill and claim whichever buffalo they wanted, so Uncle stayed at the kill to keep wolves and coyotes from sharing the meat.

I rode to the village and told the widows that we had meat for them out on the prairie. Everyone likes full bellies, so the band of Pawnee that I led back to the kill were singing Uncle's praises. Yes sir, it was a happy day for the needy.

The designated village swimming hole belongs to the women and girls after the men and boys are through with it each morning, and the men and boys had departed for their day's activity. The next morning while Uncle and I were again out hunting, Grandmother, Pick-a-Coal, and Little Star returned to the lodge from the swimming hole to find that the village police had slashed our comfortable buffalo hide tepee and broken the poles. In fact, the police were still there.

"What is the meaning of this?" Grandmother screamed.

"Shunktokecha hunted buffalo without consulting the council," they replied. A warrior is allowed to hunt anything he likes except a herd of buffalo; it's a village law. There are two reasons for the law: First, food is so precious that when a herd draws near the village, the village council wants the hunt to be organized for the maximum good of all. Second, many warriors are not proficient at lone hunting, and need the added edge of close-in, off-handed buffalo hunting to support their families.

"Shunktokecha didn't hunt a herd," she yelled. "He only stumbled upon a dozen head, and he killed all but the old bulls. You didn't investigate it properly."

"Investigation duties belong to the council, and Tonka convinced the council that no hunter could kill so many buffalo without hunting a herd."

"You still don't have authority to destroy our lodge. You haven't counted enough coup." (No village policeman can destroy the lodge of a person who has counted more coup than he.)

"Everyone has counted more coup than Shunktokecha, as he hasn't counted any," they replied.

"This lodge doesn't belong to my son, and none of you have counted more coup than my husband, Gray Wolf." It was true. Grandfather Gray Wolf had lost his scalp on his ninth coup counting expedition. He wasn't as young as the other warriors on the expedition, but he wanted to earn a war bonnet. It takes ten successful coup counting expeditions to earn a war bonnet.

Still, the lodge was already destroyed, leaving nothing for Grandmother to do but commence making a wigwam. Even with Uncle claiming the hides from all the animals he killed, it would take over a moon to cure them. It takes an entire morning of hard work just to scrape the meat and fat off each hide before you start tanning.

When Uncle and I rode in the next day, we just sat there on our mounts, amazed at the destruction. As Grandmother explained what had happened, anger mounted within me as I recalled my Missouri home that had been destroyed by the mobsters. I had made up my mind that it would never happen again, at least not without my counting coup.

Maybe I was just a savage boy of fifteen summers, yet I was born in the Moon of Wild Cherries (September), making me almost sixteen. Since I had flattened Gray Owl at age ten, and had realized that my upper body strength gave me an edge, I had prided myself on my strength. Among the boys my age, my strength was well known. But Tonka, the culprit, was four years older than I, and a warrior.

I slid off my mount and walked deliberately toward Tonka's lodge. My moves were cold and calculated, and there was purpose in every step.

"Knife Thrower!" White Rabbit yelled as she half trotted beside me, trying to keep up. "What are you doing? I don't like that look in your eyes!"

"I'm going after a mobster," I said, barely aware that she was speaking. "A black-faced mobster who needs a whipping." Everyone in the village knew the story . . . knew how Tonka had told the council only half the truth.

"You're not going after Tonka, are you?" she asked. "He's a warrior, a scalp-carrying warrior. He'll kill you!"

"I doubt it," I said. "But if I die, I die."

Ahead of me, Tonka was stepping from his lodge, mindful that he had stirred up a hornet's nest with Shunktokecha, Grandmother, and me, yet he seemingly considered only himself. It was obvious that he was prepared for a battle, as he carried a stone knife, and in his belt was a tomahawk. You don't carry a heavy stone tomahawk when just lounging around the village, because it isn't particularly comfortable hanging from your belt.

Suddenly a calico horse was blocking my path. I looked up into Uncle's cold eyes as he sat squarely astride the animal.

"He's mine, Knife Thrower, all mine. Would you take him from me?"

"What do you mean, yours?" I asked, honestly confused.

"This is my fight, and Tonka is mine to whip."

"But Uncle, you never fight anyone!" I wailed.

"That doesn't mean I can't! I'm not counting coup! As you white-eyes would say, I'm spanking a wayward child."

"Indian's don't spank children," I interjected.

"Indians can learn," he shrugged. "Besides, I have learned a few things from you about fighting, and maybe I want to see if they work. The worst thing that can happen is that I get whipped, or maybe killed. No one cares."

"Someone cares, Uncle. I care."

Turning his full attention to Tonka, Uncle slipped his left leg over his calico and slid off the animal's back. In one smooth move he slipped out of his buckskin shirt. His muscles rippled as he moved, evidence that hunting is hard work. Once a hunter kills his prey, he has to set his mind and back to carrying the carcass to the village.

A tribal elder stepped forward, flanked by several of the village policemen. "No!" he said to Tonka. "You will not kill a hunter, because the widows would suffer." Apparently it was a foregone conclusion that Tonka would be victorious. It seemed to me that the tribe held scalp-carrying warriors in more awe than they deserved. Still, the police relieved both men of their weapons.

The only thing Indians like better than story telling and trading is a good fight, and now it seemed as if the whole village was on hand, standing shoulder to shoulder, the little ones peering out from between the legs of the adults. Chatter ground to a halt, and it seemed that even Earth Mother held her breath; only the buzzing of insects disturbed the stillness.

As agile as two cats, the warrior and the hunter circled, appraising each other with steely black eyes. Uncle feigned, testing his opponent, but Tonka did the same. Uncle stepped in, but Tonka was too quick for him, sweeping Uncle off his feet in one fluid move that brought shouts of approval from his supporters. Uncle went down, but didn't stop moving as he made a complete backwards somersault, bringing grunts of pleasure from his supporters. I hadn't realized how many supporters Uncle had, though he was a likeable man, attending to the physical and emotional needs of the needy.

Again the men circled. Tonka feigned, but followed through with a solid foot to Uncle's groin. Uncle's eyes seemed to glaze for a moment, and that was long enough for Tonka to send him sprawling flat on his back. I winced, wishing it was me taking the punishment rather than him.

Uncle's recovery wasn't as fast this time, but moments later the two men were again circling. I had the impression that Uncle was stalling, letting the pain subside as he caught his breath. A third time Tonka feigned, but was caught flat-footed as he took Uncle's kick to his heart. Before he could recover, it was followed by a second to his wind. The only boxing Indians do is with their feet, as hands are reserved for holding their weapons.

Uncle stepped in, rolling Tonka off his hip, then did a complete somersault over the warrior and sprung around like a cat. The crowd looked puzzled, then roared their approval.

Tonka saw his opportunity and butted, a very logical tactic when you want to keep both feet on the ground and your hands free for slashing with a knife, as he was practiced in doing. But Uncle took the steam out of Tonka's butt with an easy backwards step, then met it with a white man's Liverpool kiss, followed by a close-in left and right to the heart with his fists. Tonka staggered. It appeared that nothing in his experience had prepared him to take a whipping like Uncle was giving him. Yet he was still on his feet, and Indian custom says you have to fall to the ground and lie still to admit defeat.

Uncle looked good, dancing around Tonka while the glaze dropped from Tonka's eyes, as only in life-and-death fights do warriors issue the death blow to a dazed opponent. Tonka still had time to fall to the ground, but he staggered, gathering his composure as the villagers roared their approval. All Indians like a good fight, even when their candidate is getting licked. Still, I was amazed at Uncle's supporters. Though some thought he was a coward for not taking scalps, they still seemed to like him.

Tonka bent over, and when he came up he had a handful of

dirt that he threw at Uncle, intending to get it in his opponent's eyes. Uncle guessed Tonka's strategy and turned his head, but he still took Tonka's foot in his kidney.

Uncle spun on around, slapping Tonka's extended leg as he spun, which pivoted Tonka on his other leg, his back to Uncle. With two hands Uncle sunk his fingers into Tonka's long greasy hair, squatted slightly as he pulled Tonka's lean frame upward, then shouldered him like a deer and started spinning.

Again the crowd roared their approval and some gave war cries as they witnessed Tonka being thoroughly whipped and thrown to the dirt, where he admitted defeat by lying still.

Generally, in Indian thinking, might means right. So the villagers looked upon Uncle with new admiration as he walked down to the village swimming hole for a cleansing dip after the fight.

Several old men lingered, looking bewildered, but one mused aloud in my hearing, "If we had allowed them to use weapons, Shunktokecha would have killed Tonka."

"Yes," replied the second. "It's rumored that Tonka purposely gave an incorrect report to the council, but he has nothing of value to make amends to Herb Woman for the destruction of her lodge, except his pony. If the council rules that Tonka should give his pony to Herb Woman, then Tonka will have to spend more evenings in the village, and we'll have to deal with his crankiness."

"Ho-o-o-o (Amen)," said the first.

"It is rumored," said the second, "that Shunktokecha has great medicine. With the sole help of Knife Thrower, he killed nine large buffaloes. No ordinary hunter could have done that. You know that we, the council, listen to him when he advises us to move the village for better hunting."

"Ho-o-o-o. The Great Spirit favors him, and so do the villagers. Most of the villagers were cheering for him even when they thought he was a loser. But when he paints his body, he uses the marking of the Sioux. He has been with the Pawnee since his twelfth summer, and should be wearing the marking of our people."

The two elders drifted away, unaware that I had been listening. But I had been thinking the same thing.

I met Gray Owl at the swimming hole where he and I planned to join Uncle in a refreshing swim. "Shunktokecha uses his hands for clubs, like you," Gray Owl observed.

"Uncle does not have to carry a knife in his hands when he fights because he doesn't plan on killing his opponent," I explained, "so he has his hands free to use as clubs. And I don't fill my hands with a knife because it is just as easy to leave my throwing knife in its sheath until I am ready to throw it."

Gray Owl grunted. "They are calling Shunktokecha a medicine man, saying that he talks with the animals."

"Maybe he does . . . I don't know. He seems to understand their ways."

Grandmother went back to making her wigwam, as the fact remained that our tepee had been destroyed. But Uncle was not satisfied. We went among those he had supplied with meat over the years, and collected surplus buffalo hides. Not only that, he secured a commitment from the women and girls to help Grandmother stitch a new tepee. It takes about twenty hides to make a tepee, though that leaves a lot of material left over, as a tepee is not the shape of buffalo hides. The excess material was retained by the providers to be used for moccasins, as the life of a moccasin is only a week.

Had the destruction taken place when we were camped on the open prairie, Grandmother would have bound the broken tepee poles with strips of rawhide and made them do. As it was, the needy of the village cut new poles for Grandmother, as Uncle's time was better spent hunting than cutting lodge poles.

COUNTING COUP

AUTUMN WAS SPENT on the plains, and we had already made the move and had our final large buffalo hunts. Autumn and winter were usually spent on the plains rather than in the forest, though it would clearly have been nice to be in the forest for firewood. But in the big autumn hunt, each lodge is stocked with their winter's supply of meat—better than a thousand pounds, much of it dried, plus many hides. With that much weight to haul, it's easier to depend on buffalo chips for most of your cooking fuel than to drag your possessions back to the trees.

With the lodges stocked for the winter, warriors have time to lie around, thinking of maidens. Naturally when they think of maidens they have to think about counting coup, as it's tradition that no Pawnee maiden will consider marrying a warrior who can't show evidence that he can protect her.

It was my sixteenth autumn, and the men of the tribe started pleading with the medicine men for a spiritual sign that a coup counting expedition against the Sioux would be successful. Even the middle-aged men wanted to go, gaining prestige in the tribe as they progressed toward their war bonnets. Fact is, all the young and middle-aged men, except Uncle, wanted to count coup.

The war priest looked into a mixture of buffalo and badger blood, and saw a Crow face rather than a Sioux face. So it was taken as a sign to count coup on the Crow.

I had grown into a tall man, standing head and shoulders above others my age. I'm sorry to say that I desperately wanted to join the war party, not only because our tribe's hatred for the Crow was repeatedly pounded into every Pawnee's head, but because I wanted an eagle feather so that I could court White Rabbit. Of course I was well under the marrying age; but a man thinks, and prepares.

Gray Owl said he was going on the expedition, and that cinched it in my mind. I had not been through my passage rites from boyhood to manhood, as had Gray Owl, but I surely wasn't going to be left behind.

Anyone can attend the scalp dance, though clearly it is designed to prepare the warrior for the glory and rigors of the war party. I joined in with the rest, dancing and slashing the air with my tomahawk . . . I had the spirit. White Rabbit paid special attention to me, as did Grandmother. I was as much a warrior as the rest, and I knew it.

The next morning I presented myself with the rest of the warriors, wearing the war paint of the Pawnee and proud of it. The final songs, embraces from wives and maidens . . . it was grand and glorious. But in the midst of my hour of glory, Grandmother crossed the warrior's ranks and marched toward me. Though a foot shorter than I, she grabbed my right ear with a fist of iron, and fairly stood me on my tiptoes as she led me out of the circle.

Though I was a strong man, it never occurred to me to fight back, not against Grandmother. Fact is, nothing I had been taught by the white or Indian cultures permitted it. The crowd roared with laughter, but I can't say that I was humiliated as much as I was disappointed. Still, as the villagers parted ranks to allow our passage, my eyes briefly caught the eyes of White Rabbit, and I shrank with shame.

Into our lodge I was pushed, and there I sat alone, Grandmother standing guard. I sat there, a big overgrown boy, nursing my feelings like a child. In my heart I thought to curse

God, but suddenly I was pleading with him. In the distance I could tell when the war party departed, as the songs of praises from the women changed to whimpers of personal loss and sorrow. Seldom had all the warriors returned; someone was always missing.

As I sat there, White Rabbit timidly parted the buffalo hump door and, like a shadow, slipped inside. Clutching what I took for a coyote pelt, she seated herself beside me, saying nothing. It felt good to have her there, but even better when she slid so close that we touched. I cast her a sidelong glance, and she gently placed her hand on my knee.

"Knife Thrower," she began, so softly I had to strain to hear, "none of us has the right to tell the gods what *they* want us to be."

Surprised, I looked deep into her black eyes, wondering what she was telling me.

"You think Ti-rá-wa didn't want me to go?" I asked.

"I . . . I don't know about Ti-rá-wa," she said, "but Herb Woman and Shunk don't want you to go."

"Without counting coup I can be a man, but I'm not a real warrior. Maidens don't take warriors seriously if they haven't counted coup."

"Maybe it's not as important as we think, Knife Thrower.

59

Shunk provides meat for many families. He's kind and gentle. We need warriors to protect us, but we need other things, too."

"I honor Uncle, but he's not respected by the warriors of the tribe."

"True, but when you are hungry, you don't consider the number of coup a warrior has counted. You consider your belly. For many years Shunk has provided meat for our lodge."

"But Uncle can't ask a maiden to marry him because he hasn't counted coup."

"Knife Thrower," she said, emphasizing my name, "Shunk hasn't asked. Though my cousin Two Kettles is older than he, she would marry him if he would court her. And Blue Star is in love with him. Everyone knows it! Everyone, that is, but Shunk."

"Blue Star?" I questioned. "She's only two summers older than we are."

"Ho," White Rabbit replied, "but Shunk is only nine summers older than we. Nine summers meant so much when we were children, but now that we are grown, it doesn't mean anything."

I grinned. "It is against our custom for a man to marry without counting coup."

"Customs can be broken," she replied. "Warriors think coup counting is so important, but the only value it has is to demonstrate that the warrior will be successful when fighting for his family. I think Blue Star thinks Shunk will fight, when the cause is right. Besides, if Shunk were a medicine man, he would not have to count coup. Everyone knows he talks to the animals. Will you speak to him?"

"Ho, I will speak with him. Is it for Blue Star that I speak?"

"Yes. She does not think that Shunk knows she exists."

"Shunk knows she exists. After all, she is a Sioux, captured as a child."

"I didn't know that," White Rabbit said.

"I am not sure that Blue Star even knows it, because according to Shunk she was very young."

"I . . . I also came to give you this," White Rabbit offered, timidly opening the pelt. It was a coyote hat, similar to Uncle's. She slid it into my hand and I fingered it reverently, examining the fine stitching. The face of the coyote was sewn into the front of the cap, and the cape dangled behind.

"It's beautiful," I said.

"I hope," she said, "it reminds you of the man I want you to be."

"You mean you want me to be like Uncle?"

"Of course, stupid," she teased.

MEDICINE MAN

I TALK WITH MEMBERS of the animal tribe," Uncle said when I questioned him, "but they do not answer me. Sometimes I think they understand what I am saying. I understand them. Sometimes they would have spoken with me had they had it in them to speak with man.

"My Sioux father was a medicine man and wanted me to follow his ways, teaching me much, as did your grandmother, Herb Woman. My life changed when I spoke with the Nephite prophet, but I think I could serve Wakan Tonka better were I a medicine man." Wakan Tonka means Great Spirit; it's Sioux, as Uncle was Sioux, and he always used Sioux words when referring to deity.

There are nearly as many kinds of medicine men in the Indian culture as there are medicine men. Yet all medicine men or women need to be properly inducted with a bear ceremony, preceded by a personal vision-seeking experience.

"It is time, Knife Thrower, for you to have your first hanblechia (vision-seeking)," Uncle observed. The first hanblechia was also a rite of passage from boyhood to manhood. It was Grandmother's place to say when I was ready, though she was bound to accept Uncle's suggestion, as he was my trainer. Had I already had my hanblechia, Grandmother would not have kept me from joining the war party, though now that the fervor of its departure was over, it didn't pain me so keenly. "I, too, shall have a hanblechia," Uncle continued, "and seek the will of the Great Mystery."

The prospect of at last achieving adulthood triggered a thrill of achievement within my soul, yet it seemed that I was in a dream. Uncle and I set about making preparations by first making kinnickinnick, a tobacco made from the bark of the red willow and used for the purification ceremony. We would be spending four days smoking, fasting, and praying.

Next, Uncle had me find two gourds for rattles, which were made using tiny rocks from ant hills that were said to have great powers. No one knows why ants gather the little rocks—no one but the gods.

As I swished aside the buffalo hump door to our lodge, gourds in hand, there sat Grandmother. Blood was dripping off the end of her left elbow, and in her right hand she held a flint knife. Beside her on a hunk of bark were many tiny pieces of flesh. I knew there were exactly forty, or would be when Grandmother was finished, and that she had painfully cut them from her arm. I don't know why the number is forty, neither does Grandmother, but I suspect it has something to do with Christ fasting for forty days, and the bits of flesh are akin to the sacrament. Still, the sight of her bloody arm made me angry, as it was a weird old custom that I surely didn't adhere to.

"Grandmother!" I scolded, "I told you I didn't want that!"

"It is our way," she defended herself as she laid aside her knife.

"Our ways can change, Grandmother."

"If I didn't sacrifice the flesh, Knife Thrower, how would Ti-rá-wa and the villagers know that I loved you?" There was a little hole in the waist of her dress, made by an accidental slip of a knife when the hide was being scraped for tanning. When Grandmother was nervous she'd slip her long finger into the hole and sort of wring it. Even as I spoke, she was wringing the hole. Her lips were quivering and she was half biting her lower lip. Her eyes glistened through a face that was wrinkled as a prune.

I plopped down beside her and drew her to me, careful not to touch her bloody arm. She allowed me to hold her, but a shiver ran through her frail frame. Sometimes, amongst the family, Indians show nearly as much emotion as do whites.

"Everyone knows you love me, Grandmother. Given half a chance, you brag about everything I do. But putting forty pieces of dried flesh in a rattle is a custom that the younger parents are starting to abandon. It seems too much like human sacrifice."

"Did you not tell us the story of your God giving his followers pieces of his flesh to eat?"

"That was just bread, given to represent his flesh."

"I don't see much difference, Knife Thrower. Those are just tiny pieces of flesh that represent me, when you and Shunk make your rattles."

"Regardless," I said, "don't you ever do it again!"

"But I'm the grandmother and you are the child. You're not supposed to chastise me."

"I'll only be a child for four more days, Grandmother."

"Ho-o-o-o," she said, and was content to let me hold her for a moment. Then placing one hand on my face and fingering my beard, which was starting to get long, she looked into my eyes and remarked, "Some maidens are starting to ridicule you for having hair on your face. They say you look like a bear, and should be named 'Bear Face.'"

"Does White Rabbit ridicule me?"

"I have not heard her, but I am sure she doesn't care for it, as no Pawnee maiden does. White men used to scare me because some of them had hair on their faces, but you don't scare me. Still, in the spring I think you should travel to the paleface and buy a knife that shaves."

"I don't have any paleface money to buy it with."

"It is said that the paleface will sell anything for gold. I have a little gold I will give you."

It was important that we select a period of favorable weather for the vision-seeking . . . not as much for me as for Uncle. If lightning struck the hill, it would be a sign that Uncle's bid as a medicine man was against the will of the Great Mystery, and he would be turned into a contrarywise man . . . a clown. But it was Indian summer, and we thought the weather would hold.

After a cleansing swim the day of our vision-seeking, three medicine men joined Uncle and me in the sweat lodge. In the fire ring, old Crooked Teeth, the patriarch of the medicine men, had prepared a stack of red-hot stones. Old Crooked Teeth had seemed scary when I was a lad, because whenever he spoke his words seemed to whistle through his teeth. When the five of us were crowded into the lodge, Crooked Teeth secured the entrance, then proceeded to pour water over the stones as he sang, "Oh holy rocks, we receive your white breath, the steam. It is thy breath. Let us all inhale it and make us strong." He was joined by Uncle and the other medicine men. When finished, the four of them proceeded to chant the chants of the old one, a lost language that only the medicine men understood. The process continued until there was no steam given off when water was poured over the rocks.

It seemed that every ounce of strength was thoroughly sapped out of our bodies, then we were led for miles to our separate vision-seeking sites. Mine was a hole in the side of a rise where I would be safe from predators that might want to take advantage of my weakened state, and visit me for dinner. For my protection, a woven willow shield was placed over my hole. There I huddled, smoked my ceremonial pipe of kinnickinnick, and felt light-headed. When it seemed as if evil lurked in the darkness, I would rattle my rattle, which was supposed to drive the evil spirit away. It seemed to work, and the rattle was a comfort to me.

What I experienced and dreamed in my four days and three nights of fasting was sacred and personal. I dreamed of my paleface and Lamanite families, and in my dreams I even saw Christ visiting the temple in Bountiful.

It was the fourth day, at least I thought it was the fourth day. Old Crooked Teeth hissed, "Knife Thrower, are you there?"

"Yes, Crooked Teeth," I weakly replied.

"The time is completed. Have you seen a vision?"

"I saw many visions and dreamed many dreams, Crooked Teeth."

"Come tell me about them," he directed.

Slowly I crawled from my hole, and saw that Crooked Teeth was putting together a fire. He handed me a container of water and watched me closely, seeing if I would gorge myself or take only tiny sips, allowing my stomach to stretch. I took tiny sips.

"You have done well," Crooked Teeth said as he handed me some cold venison. I ate slowly, chewing every mouthful well, as one does when he has been without food for a long time.

Crooked Teeth had me rehearse every detail of my vision-seeking. Nodding, he listened intently as I passed from one item to the next. It was dark when he arose and, placing one outstretched arm on my shoulder, declared, "You have done well, Knife Thrower. When you return to the village in the morning, you may move your belongings to the warrior's lodge." Nothing more was spoken, and I was left alone, but not for long, as Uncle, looking as worn and tired as I, stepped into my circle of light from the darkness. We embraced, then extinguished the fire and moved off into the darkness to bed down. In the morning we would wash, observe the Great Silence (an individual morning devotional), then I would enter the village for my first time as an adult.

EAGLE FEATHER

EVERY AUTUMN, one or more enemy war parties either attacked our village or raided our horse herd. No two raids were alike, and we were always concerned that the enemy's cunning might be greater than our own.

Uncle was sleeping to my left about the span of three lodges, for better defense. When two Indians are away from the village, they never sleep next to each other unless it's winter and they need each other's body warmth. Neither of us slept well, as the water and food we had been given upon completion of our vision-seeking did not meet our cravings.

Overhead, the harvest moon was large and yellow. Most Indians don't care much for doing anything at night, as night is considered inhabited by spirits. They especially don't like fighting at night because the spirits of departed warriors can wander, becoming lost. But in the pre-dawn darkness, Indians often slip unseen into position for an early dawn attack. For some mysterious reason unknown to me, Uncle was not hampered by the Indian's usual aversion to the darkness.

I saw Uncle turn over and was about to call out, suggesting to him that we hike the mile to the creek for a drink, when I heard something moving in the buffalo grass. I froze. The sound came again. I looked at Uncle, and saw only the tip of his bow. Guessing he had an arrow fit to the string, I did the same.

Uncle is one of the few Indians who sight a bow most of the time. Don't get me wrong, anyone with a bow in his hands can sight it; but if your arrows won't fly true beyond twenty paces, you use off-handed shooting. Uncle uses only the finest arrows, made from long-grain wood not found on the plains.

Few white people realize that Indians have a trading system sufficient to allow plains tribes to buy long-grain wood, which doesn't grow on or near the plains. A trader can literally go anywhere . . . a trader and a peaceful medicine man . . . and most mountain men are considered traders by the Indians. So Uncle had acquired some mighty fine arrows, and wasn't about to wound an animal and take a chance of losing one of his arrows. If he let an arrow fly, the game was as good as dead. 'Course he didn't shoot men, but if he had he would have cut his arrow out of the man's dead body, not just pull it out, as he might pull off the arrowhead and have to repair the arrow before using it again.

Well, I followed Uncle's example and fit an arrow into my bow. Then I waited, gradually making out what was moving.

It was two Indians—scouts, no doubt. There were two kinds of scouts: a war scout and a hunting scout. A hunting scout doesn't wander around in the middle of the night, so we assumed the Indians were war scouts. Apparently they had already scouted our village and were returning to their war party to report their findings, and naturally they didn't expect us to be where we were. Of course I didn't blame them, as we were far beyond normal village sentry lines, but much too close for hunters who had gotten stranded for the night away from the village.

As the men drew closer, it looked to me as if they were going to walk right over me. This was the real thing! Though I had been looking forward to counting coup just a few weeks earlier, my mouth was dry and I had to steel myself to keep from shaking.

Closer they came. I had my bow aimed toward the heart of the lead warrior, as Uncle had trained me to sight a bow. 'Course I could shoot off-hand, as could Uncle, but I had high-quality arrows too, and didn't want to lose them.

I still couldn't tell the tribe of the Indians, but they were obviously enemies. As the lead Indian came within a dozen paces of me, he must have seen something because he suddenly went for his bow. He was too slow. My arrow flew true, right to his heart.

Warriors train themselves not to cry out. The only bad thing about this is that occasionally, if a warrior cried out when he was shot, his cry would alert his buddies. As it was, the second warrior, walking ten paces behind the first, didn't know why the lead warrior stumbled, then fell. He fit an arrow to his bow, but it didn't do him any good. Uncle's arrow caught the scout in the chest. It wasn't a straight-on shot, as Uncle was at an angle to him. But as the scout raised to his tiptoes, Uncle's second arrow caught him in the throat.

We listened for anyone else, then after a reasonable period we worked ourselves to the two dead scouts. They bore the feathers and wore the war paint of the Crow. Possibly a hundred miles from the nearest Crow village, we had obviously killed two scouts of a Crow war party, intent on counting coup on our village.

We each scalped the warrior we had killed, then very quietly counted coup. The ceremony for counting coup is nearly the same in every plains tribe: "I, Knife Thrower, brave Pawnee warrior, count first coup on my enemy the Crow. Uncle is my witness." When the Nephite prophet told Uncle not to count coup, he used the word for counting coup that meant murder for sport—something quite different from defending yourself or your village.

"The Crow war party is obviously behind us," Uncle whispered, "else the scouts wouldn't have been making their way this direction in the dark. Do you think you can run to the village and alert them?"

"I don't know where our village sentry line is, Uncle," I hesitated, not wanting to get myself killed by Pawnee sentries. "I can creep close and give the call, and hope they answer."

"When you get close, give the call every few minutes, though they won't answer until they recognize you, thinking it might be a trick. If need be, remain motionless until it gets gray in the sunrise."

"Where are you going?"

"I'm going to scout around."

"Be careful, Uncle. You're a hunting scout, not a war scout."

"I'll be careful," he replied, "though there's no finer way to die than in defending your village."

"Uncle Coyote!" I exclaimed, as Uncle's full name, Shunktokecha, means coyote, "I'm not ready to take on meat-hunting duties for the whole family!"

He grinned, touching his hat. "With my coyote hat, I might even be taken for a coyote."

Even in my weakened conditioned I ran, putting two miles behind me in no time. When within half a mile of the village, I slowed to a walk and gave three hoots of the fledgling owl, the most alarming of the Indian distress signals. It's an almost human sound, like the crying of a distressed child.

There was no response. I repeated the distress signal every fifty feet as I walked upright in the light of the moon, so that I would easily be recognized. Suddenly a sentry appeared, almost at my side, followed by a second. In their bows were fixed arrows.

"It's me," I whispered, "Knife Thrower!" They seemed to relax a little.

"Why do you give the alarm so early in the morning?" a sentry asked.

I produced my fresh Crow scalp and a Crow eagle feather. "Uncle and I killed two Crow scouts, coming from the direction of our village."

Both sentries examined the scalp and the feather. "Rush to the village and alert the war chief," one sentry directed. "We will alert the other sentries."

I trotted into the village to the yammer of foxes, though they weren't real foxes but sentries. Once in the village, I slapped the side of Eagle Eyes' lodge and gave three hoots of an owl. Eagle

Eyes was the war chief. He burst through his buffalo hide door with such speed that you would have thought he had been lying wide awake, waiting for me. Instantly he recognized me, but his face remained stoic. I mutely offered him the bloody scalp and Crow eagle feather, which he examined with care in the moonlight, then cast me a questioning glance.

"Uncle and I killed two Crow scouts," I explained, "two, maybe three miles over there." I pointed in the direction I had come.

"Where is Shunktokecha now?" he asked.

"He is playing the role of war scout, waiting to see if they will attack when their scouts fail to return." He grunted thoughtfully. There are many things that will keep scouts from returning on time, but if a war party finds that two scouts have been killed, they might think the gods no longer favor their attack, and will wait a day or two, seeking new guidance from their war priest. Yet you couldn't count on it.

"Alert the village," he ordered. Almost as an after-thought he added, "Please allow me to retain the scalp and feather for a few hours to exhibit to the elders."

To alert the village, my duty was to slap each tepee lightly and give three of anything: hoots of an adult owl, calls of a quail, yips of a fox, anything. It took quite a while as there were many lodges. To an outsider there was very little movement, but in reality shields were positioned, weapons were attended to, and peekholes were opened up along the rear tepee seams. Many warriors slipped from their lodges like shadows and took up positions in the buffalo grass, their shields before them. War scouts slipped out of the village on their scouting duties.

As day broke, the village seemingly remained asleep. The Great Silence came and went, but no one moved. Only when the sun was a hand high in the sunrise sky did the village start to come to life, satisfied that the attack had at least been delayed. Eagle Eyes displayed the fresh scalp and Crow feather on a lance in front of his lodge, which told the story with very little explanation. Still, the village was uneasy as they waited for word from the war scouts.

It wasn't until the sun was three hands high that the advance scouts rode in, reporting that a rider resembling Shunktokecha was driving a small herd of horses to the village. Waiting, wondering, eagerly anticipating Uncle's story, we all studied the prairie. Sure enough, the herd of seven mounts appeared, driven by Uncle. Even more amazing, they were mostly calico horses, a favorite of Uncle's, though one was a tall roan gelding wearing horseshoes. The roan was the prettiest horse I had ever seen.

As the villagers gathered around him, Uncle bucked his horse to a halt. Sort of casual-like, he dumped seven fresh scalps to the dirt, then just sat on his mount, relaxed, watching the expressions of his fellow villagers. It was a real show, and he had everyone's attention.

"It was a Crow war party of thirty-one warriors," he began. "They were camped in a low spot by the stream. Seems a coyote slipped in and one by one picked off their sentries, then hazed out eight mounts."

"Why only eight?" someone asked.

"Well," he reasoned, "if that coyote had taken all their mounts, then the Crow would have been forced to attack, or they would have had to walk a hundred miles back home, afoot. As it was, they found eight dead warriors, so they knew their medicine had gone sour, but they still had enough mounts to return home."

"We could have taken them," one young warrior offered.

"Maybe you could, maybe you couldn't," Uncle replied, "but we'll get farther convincing them that war against our village is bad medicine than by fighting hand-to-hand battles."

"I'm surprised there were so many calico horses in one herd," I observed to Uncle when we were alone.

"There weren't all that many," Uncle replied. "I had killed the guard, so I chose the horses I wanted. Medicine men like to ride calico ponies." He cast me a curious sidelong glance. "I chose the tall roan for you, Knife Thrower, because you're tall and need a tall horse. After all, we worked as a team."

THE BEAR DANCE

U NCLE WAS NOW a respected man around the village, eligible to wear seven eagle feathers with round marks cut into them and painted red, which meant that he counted coup, slew his enemy, and lifted his enemy's scalp. You can count coup without killing your enemy if you have a witness, but without a witness you have to take the enemy's scalp as proof.

I was eligible to wear one eagle feather, though neither Uncle nor I had a ready source of them, as eagles don't just swoop down to the earth and say, "Here, Knife Thrower, have a feather." Fact is, eagles are about as selfish over parting with a feather as a Crow warrior is about parting with his top knot (scalp).

To get an eagle feather you have to dig a hole large enough for you to huddle in, cover it with a willow mat that you can reach through, then place a dead rabbit on top as bait. 'Course you have to anchor the rabbit good and keep wiggling it from underneath to attract the eagle's attention. And it helps to have your hand and arm wrapped in leather, though even that is scary, as an eagle can tear most leather with its beak. Warriors usually use the thick leather from the hump of a buffalo. When the eagle swoops down and latches onto the rabbit, you reach out and swipe a feather, maybe two.

Still, I already had a small, battered eagle feather, such as it was. I had found it as a boy and tucked it into my boyhood treasure pouch, as I wasn't eligible to wear it then, and it was of poor quality. I could wear it until I got something better.

Being a warrior wasn't Uncle's goal, not by a long ways. He had a couple of feathers, but he didn't bother putting them in his hair. Still, I had spoken with him about Blue Star, and it seemed to brighten his day. He started wearing a breastwork of porcupine quills which, according to Pick-a-Coal, Blue Star made for him.

The next day the village crier announced a Bear Dance (a religious rite in honor of Uncle becoming a medicine man, and I joined in the task of digging a bear den a hundred paces from the village. We dug the hole about eighteen inches deep, then built a wickiup on top which was open on four sides.

Women don't participate in Bear Dances unless they are being inducted as medicine women; then they take the role of the bear. Usually they just watch and cheer. Of course women and men never dance together in any type of dance, though a Bear Dance is not like a scalp dance or a victory dance. When it's all over, we have a dance around the fire.

The day of the dance it was gray and overcast, though not cold. It looked as if our long Indian summer was ending. The feathered tribes were all making their way south, signaling impending winter.

I suppose that every inch of my body was painted, or close to it, as were the bodies of the other villagers who were going to participate. It was my first opportunity to wear my eagle feather. Uncle was crouched in his bear den, his face painted like his Sioux medicine man father might paint his, and he wore a bear cape. He was probably excited, because a Bear Dance is not only religious, it's fun. Dutifully we kept our distance until the tomtom summoned us to circle the den.

The significance of that part of the dance was a prophecy of things to come. On the signal from an elder, the men and boys would approach the bear and try to touch him without being touched. If they succeeded, it was assumed that they also would succeed in battle. But if the bear touched them back, it was assumed that they would fail in battle. On the next coup counting expedition, only those joined the war party who had not been touched by the bear; but chances were good that only the warrior and the bear would know if the warrior had been touched. If a warrior got careless and accidentally tripped, it was assumed that he or a close relative would suddenly die. Boys and men alike participated. Knowing Uncle, he would endeavor to touch the whole village, 'cause as many as he touched were not likely to go out on the next war party, which meant they wouldn't get themselves killed, leaving their widows and families for the hunters to support.

The elder gave the signal for the first round of taunting the bear, and we all cautiously approached. It didn't pay to rush head-on until you saw how quick the bear was. If you were anxious to count coup in battle, it was better to wait for the bear to tire before attempting to touch him, lest he be too quick for you.

On the third round I very nearly tripped, which frightened me. Though I was Christian and a Mormon, I wasn't sure what means God used to communicate with man . . . not all his means, anyway. It was only with great difficulty that I kept from falling, and when it was over my heart was racing and I was shaking.

I noticed that White Rabbit's little brother, Fleet-of-Foot, was daring and cocky, but it didn't seem that he had much to lose because he wasn't going on a war party, not in the near future anyway. As far as that goes, I no longer desired to join a war party, and was a little ashamed of myself for ever wanting to, being a Mormon and all.

On the fifth round, Fleet-of-Foot touched the bear, but Uncle sprinted to touch the little warrior before he made it across the line. Suddenly Fleet-of-Foot tripped and landed flat on his face, and Uncle almost fell over him.

Instantly everyone was quiet, contemplating. Not a soul spoke. Even the insects stopped buzzing, though from somewhere high above a Canadian goose honked. White Rabbit stepped forward timidly and helped Fleet-of-Foot to his feet, as she, being a girl, was immune to the touch of the bear. Though not a little boy, Fleet-of-Foot seemed small and pitiful. His eyes were red, so I unconsciously looked away, fearing the boy might cry.

A high-pitched death chant rent the air, and everyone cast their eyes to its source, Fleet-of-Foot's mother. She was mourning for her older son, Gray Owl, somewhere in Crow country on a war party. All agreed that Gray Owl would soon die.

"Not Gray Owl!" Fleet-of-Foot gasped, choking on his own words. Then the tears came to his eyes . . . not many, as he was struggling to be a man. Yet he cried, and everyone saw it. With White Rabbit's arms around him, he made his way to his family's lodge and disappeared inside.

We returned to our Bear Dance, but an hour later the air was again rent with a death cry. Fleet-of-Foot had died. Maybe he had died of a broken heart, who knows? But he had gone to live with his ancestors beyond the Great River, or maybe he went to live with Jesus like Mama and Papa. Jesus would take a Pawnee boy who cried, wouldn't he?

The winter storms had arrived, and with them came the return of the war party. At least most of them returned. Before they were close enough to the village for us to tell who was returning, we knew seven didn't make it. Seven were left behind in Crow country, buried Pawnee style.

My heart in my throat, I strained to see if my friend Gray Owl was in the group. I recognized his silhouette as he rode. Beside me, White Rabbit jumped with delight. He rode up stoic and proper, with an air of pride. Yet later I learned that he came home somewhat disappointed. He had shot an enemy, but when he snaked up to the dead foe, all he found was blood. The Crow's friends had spirited him away before Gray Owl could scalp count coup. Still, Gray Owl had shown his bravery, something necessary for courting.

The village air was again filled with death wails, as some of the villagers had lost husbands, some had lost lovers, and some had lost sons. Life is hard when you have to prove your manhood to court.

For the next while I lived in the warrior's lodge, at least I slept there, though many nights I slept in Grandmother's lodge. My friends were in the warrior's lodge, but when listening to them relate their stories of counting coup, I didn't get the same thrill as when I was a lad. Maybe Uncle trained it out of me, I don't know. But I kept thinking of the wives or girlfriends of the slain foes.

BLUE STAR

UNCLE WAS FAST BECOMING a legendary hunter in his own time, and he continued to bring in buffalo long after no other hunters could find them. Yet none of the needy who received the meat received the hides. There did seem to be many hides curing near Blue Star's lodge.

On the prairie, as we were, the wind howled and ground blizzards were frequent. Yet around our village was a pole windbreak, which also kept out coyote, wolves, and anything else that might lurk in the darkness. Grass had cured on the stalk, and the same wind that piled up snowdrifts also swept snow from patches of grass, which the ponies ate. Fuel was short, so the fire in the warrior's lodge was allowed to die, and the young warriors crowded in with their relatives for warmth.

"Do you want to cut poles with me, Knife Thrower?" Uncle asked one cold day. "There isn't much wind today, so a trip to the forest would be practical." Uncle well knew that unlike all other young men in the village, I did all the wood gathering and chopping for Grandmother's lodge. 'Course I had selfish motives, as it was part of my effort to keep up my upper body strength, one thing that gave me an edge over the other boys.

"I would enjoy gathering wood, but why lodge poles?"

"For the same reason Blue Star has a pile of cured buffalo hides behind her parents' lodge," he said. "Why should I waste all the lovely cold nights of winter sleeping with you,

Grandmother, and the girls, when Blue Star and I can begin our marriage and have a lovely winter honeymoon, right here in the village? Besides, in the summer you're going to Missouri with me to get the Lamanite book you're going to read to me."

"You do have a point there, Uncle," I grinned. "When are we going to go?"

"In the morning," he replied.

The roan horse that Uncle had given me was a horse made for a big man. He liked to run with the wind in his face and his mane flying. He wasn't very old, just two years according to his teeth. A horse his size is too big for most Indians, as they like to hold on by curling their short legs around the horse's belly and lying against the horse's side while riding at a full gallop, shielded from their enemies by the horse's body. That's hard to do on a big horse like the roan, unless you also have long legs, as I have.

The horse nickered as I approached with a saddle blanket and Pawnee saddle in my hand. "You have a real friend there," Uncle commented. "That big horse has taken to you."

"He's like me, a big horse among mustang ponies," I replied. "Yet he has a hint of mustang blood."

We saddled up and moved out, Uncle and I each leading two pack ponies on halter ropes. The ponies were for dragging the poles, firewood, and any game we might shoot back to camp.

On the flank of Uncle's calico pony he had painted a keyhole; at least that's how it would appear to a paleface. Actually it was a medicine man symbol, telling everyone he was a medicine man, which gave him freedom of movement among Indian villages and tribes. Below the medicine man symbol were seven coup marks, which gave him a measure of respect.

Behind our crude saddles, we each carried something new that Uncle had traded for: a Hudson Bay blanket. The traders had come to our village, trading for pelts. The blankets weren't new, but they were sound, and they weighed a lot less than buffalo robes. A buffalo robe, even when cut and trimmed for sleeping, still weighs half as much as a man. We weren't planning an overnight trip, but we still carried the blankets, as it always pays to be prepared.

Riding easy, it only took us two hours to reach the forest and another thirty minutes to reach tall, spindly stuff, suitable for lodge poles. Still, we didn't go right to chopping, as we wanted a short hunt. Once you start hacking away with your flint axes, the sound drives the game away.

Light on our feet, we moved out and found small deer tracks in the snow. During the day, deer sleep and they're hard to spot, so you have to be extremely cautious. But Uncle found the little creature, a black-tailed deer weighing about seventy-five pounds, and put an arrow in her heart. Then on the way back to where the horses were waiting, we killed a fat porcupine by rapping him on the head with a stout stick.

"What are you and Blue Star going to do for a wedding feast?" I asked as we approached the horses with our game.

"We're not going to have a wedding feast," he replied.

"You're going to elope?"

"No."

I was puzzled. Prominent families always had wedding feasts, and children of poor families eloped. There wasn't an in-between that I had seen.

"This is the Moon of Depression (January)," he reminded me. 'Course I knew that. "There will be near famine in the lodges of the poor until after the Moon of Sore Eyes (March). If we have a feast, the poor that I support will suffer." It made sense, as Indians consumed enough food in one feast to feed the poor for a month if they rationed it.

We set our backs to the job of chopping and skinning lodge poles, and I naturally thought of Blue Star as we worked. "How many horses will you give her father?" I asked. Uncle knew I was speaking of Blue Star.

"I'll offer one, then he'll demand three, and we'll probably settle on two horses and maybe a blanket."

"You can get her cheaper than two horses," I replied.

Uncle paused, looking at me hard. "Yes, but why would I want to?" he questioned. It was something to consider.

We completed our cutting, then made travoises with the poles and loaded our game and as much firewood as the ponies could drag. Then we made our way out of the forest and across the prairie. Back in our village, Uncle dumped the deer and some firewood in front of his future mother-in-law's lodge, then we rode on. It was all part of the marriage ritual, an invitation to Blue Star to demonstrate her cooking skills.

The next morning Uncle didn't eat a morning meal, expecting an invitation to eat with Blue Star. Near noon Blue Star approached with an invitation for him to eat a meal she had prepared at her parents' lodge. He accepted, and the meal must have been to his liking, as was the conversation with her father afterward, because three hours later I saw him walking through the village leading two horses.

"Would you like to go for some more firewood tomorrow?" Uncle asked that evening as we sat around Grandmother's fire.

"Sure," I grinned. "How many days will we spend?" It was a custom for the groom to go hunting or something while the women prepared the bridal lodge, usually a grass wickiup.

"Just one night," he replied. "The women I have been hunting meat for will help Blue Star stitch the lodge."

The next morning, before the Great Silence, Uncle and I were riding. I would have liked to sleep longer, but Uncle couldn't sleep. We did some hunting, collected as much firewood as the horses could handle, and when the day was over we bedded down near a campfire.

The following morning we started home, but stopped a mile out of our village by a stream for Uncle's pre-wedding bath. I thought he was going to bathe all morning. When he came out of the water he was a red man, rather than a brown man; and if

I hadn't had a warm fire blazing, he might have been a naked hunk of ice.

When we rode into the village, we dumped our firewood by a new tepee located next to Uncle's future in-laws. Pretty ritzy, I thought. Uncle was the first newlywed I had ever seen who could afford to start off his marriage in a brand new private tepee for a lodge. Most winter newlyweds spend the first few nights alone on an Indian-style honeymoon, but subsequent nights in the lodge of the bride's family. They live with the bride's family until the couple has acquired enough tanned hides for a tepee. 'Course if they're not getting along with her family, they might settle for a wigwam for a lodge.

I missed not having a wedding feast, but the whole village knew food was scarce. We met in the council lodge with as many villagers as could crowd in, and listened to the exhausting counsel from the medicine men. Then the storytelling and wedding jokes started. Blue Star and Uncle were supposed to slip off to their wedding lodge unnoticed, if they could. They failed miserably, as all were watching them slip away.

MISSOURI

AFTER THE LEAN DAYS of winter, spring brought an end to the annual famine. Our village's spring camp was always in the trees, where we feasted on the small animals of the forest—animals which would have been extinct had we tried to harvest them year-round.

Grandmother insisted that I should purchase a razor. I had noticed that White Rabbit seemed a little repulsed by my whiskers; but when I shaved, as I did now and again with my throwing knife, it would only be a day until she'd turn up her nose at my scratchy face. It seemed to me that Grandmother was expecting magic from the razor. Sure, many white men kept their faces free of whiskers, but they shaved every day. Still, I obeyed Grandmother, half expecting a miracle myself.

Not many days' journey to the east was Fort Leavenworth. Naturally the fort would have a trading post that would sell razors, or so it seemed. But Uncle reminded me that I had promised to try to secure a copy of the Book of Mormon and read it to him, if I could still read, so it looked like I was going to Missouri. 'Course I had personal motives: I wanted to see the old homesite.

I told Grandmother that I had heard more than one Missourian declare that "The only good Indian is a dead Indian," and I believed they were serious. Grandmother's solution was to make me look like a white man, so she began artistically making me some white man's leather clothes. She got the pattern from some cast-off leather mountain-man clothes that a villager had acquired along the Oregon Trail to the south of us.

All spring Grandmother repeatedly counseled me to stay away from paints, allowing my skin to return to its burned, brown complexion as much as possible. I told her that white men had a substance made from ashes and animal fat, called soap, that would remove the paint. But even as I spoke I wasn't sure of it, as some things don't wash off your skin . . . they have to wear off.

Early summer is the time for Indians to wander. Food is adequate in the lodges, and the last summer gathering season has not yet arrived. So Uncle and I prepared for our trip to Missouri. Yet in spite of our excitement over the journey, he was not anxious to leave his young wife. I've noticed that marriage often does that to warriors.

Under a rich blue sky with white cloud pillows, we made a mid-morning departure from the village. Before Uncle was married, he would have insisted on a pre-dawn departure. But now, even after we left, he glanced back a time or two.

We each led a pack animal loaded with things white men were known to covet, mainly raw pelts, as white men preferred to do their own tanning. In my possibles bag were gold nuggets from Grandmother. Uncle wanted some steel knives and arrowheads, and he was hoping I could buy him a rifle, since it was unlikely that a white man would sell a rifle to an Indian. Grandmother wanted a big cast-iron pot and a steel axe. It was unlikely that we would have the trading power to purchase everything we wanted, but we would make do with what we purchased. It's odd how Indians despise whites, yet hold them in awe. To the Indian, it seems that whites can work magic.

The prairie was shimmering with heat waves as we rode south to catch the Oregon Trail; our movement through the grass stirred the insects. My mountain-man clothes were hot and miserable, yet I kept them on, though I would have preferred a clout (a loincloth made from soft leather). Why white men dressed the way they did in the summer, I surely didn't know.

We rode until the horses began to show signs of fatigue, then we trotted a spell, leading the animals. For jogging I slipped into my clout, as every man has his limits. When we reached the Oregon Trail, we turned left. We were constantly wary, as the stories Indians tell of encounters with the pale-faces are somewhat the same as the stories palefaces tell of Indian encounters. Neither white nor Indian treats the other with much respect.

Lone wagons don't travel the Oregon or Santa Fe trails, though many Indians wished they did. Palefaces carry many things of value to Indians, but it's hard to loot wagons when palefaces travel in large numbers.

We encountered our first wagon company after we had reached the Santa Fe Trail and turned toward Independence. We could see their dust from miles away, so Uncle and I had time to ride off the trail and hide ourselves until the poky wagon train passed. We had heard tell that white people treat Indians better in their forts and towns than when they encounter lone Indians along the trail.

We had been traveling six days when we passed Westport (Kansas City) and entered Missouri. The supply stop and landing couldn't have been more than a year old, as the logs still had their fresh appearance. From there we passed small farms and occasional lone wagons. Though most of our encounters with lone wagons were genial enough, the first driver we met was clearly suspicious of us. As we approached he laid a rifle on his lap, casual like, aiming toward us. We didn't like the way he shifted nervously, so we rode to opposite sides of the wagon. 'Course he didn't like that, as he could only point his rifle one direction. He chose to point at Uncle.

"Howdy," I greeted. As I recalled, that's the way Papa used to greet strangers.

"Howdy," he replied, looking at me with hard eyes.

"How far is it to Independence?"

"Five, maybe six eye-sees to where you can sell your furs," he muttered, casting a glance at our pack animals and spitting a stream of tobacco juice into the dust. An eye-see is as far as you can see clearly, but it doesn't really tell you how far.

I glanced at a plow in the back of his wagon, and was surprised that it was so small. When I was a kid the plows seemed larger.

"Good day," I said, and nudged my mount farther to the side of the trail. I didn't turn my back on him, as it never pays to turn your back on an enemy.

"Maybe it's the hat," Uncle muttered as we continued our journey.

"What's the hat?"

"He seems suspicious of us, though you're wearing white men's clothes . . . all but your hat. I haven't seen a white man wear a coyote hat. Maybe you should tuck it into the pack."

"I hadn't thought of that," I replied, and removed the hat.

We rode on towards Independence, cautious and apprehensive. I recalled Papa saying that Independence wasn't an incorporated town like Kirtland, Palmyra, or even Far West. It was just a wide spot in Jackson County, a mighty wide spot. It had streets and blocks, and most significantly, it had a temple site, set apart by Brother Joseph. Papa said Independence and Fort Leavenworth were both settled in 1827, which I remembered because that was the year before I was born. When Fort Osage was disbanded four years earlier, Independence gradually took over the lucrative business of outfitting the westward-bound wagon trains.

As we neared Independence, we started passing scattered farms along the trail. Suddenly Uncle drew rein, gawking at the goings-on in a barnyard. A huge ox, supported in a sling, was dangling barely off the ground.

"What are the palefaces doing with that bull?" he questioned.

"It's an ox," I replied. "Off-hand, I'd say they were shoeing it."

"Shoeing it?" he questioned. "I've seen palefaces shoe horses, and that's not the way they do it. They just back themselves up to the animal, hold its foreleg between their knees, and slap on a shoe."

"True," I said, "but oxen won't stand three-legged. You have to throw them on their side, which isn't easy, or hoist them off their feet."

"Why won't they stand three-legged? They lift two legs off the ground when they walk."

"I surely don't know," I mused. "I don't recall Papa ever telling me why."

As we proceeded on, it seemed that every home had a larger garden than was needed to support the family. Fields of corn, ears not yet showing, lined the trail. It didn't take much sense to realize that farmers around Independence made their living by supplying wagon trains.

As I cast a glance at Uncle, I saw him eyeing the farmers' gardens hungrily. "Don't even consider it," I said. "Many a time I've heard Papa say that no one in Jackson County will let you pull so much as a parsnip from his garden without demanding pay. 'Cept the Mormons, and I'm not so sure about them. And when we get into the business district, Uncle, don't be fooled by the rich men who invite you into their lodges for a feast. They prepare feasts for a living, and as soon as you eat your fill they'll demand money for the food you ate."

On the outskirts of the business district was a public corral where half a dozen mountain men had collected and were sharing a jug. Nearby, horses with empty packs hinted that the men had recently sold a load of pelts. When we were within speaking distance, we pulled rein.

"We're looking for a place to sell our pelts," I explained as we steadied our mounts. A middle-aged man cast me a sidewise glance, then gave Uncle a long, appraising look. Having mountain man savvy, he glanced at the medicine and coup marks on Uncle's pony, and seemed to straighten slightly.

"Try the trading post at the far end of the street," he said to me. "They hain't pilgrims when it comes to appraising fine pelts. Rumor has it that they're secretly buying for the Hudson Bay Company, but it makes no difference to us. They'll treat you right, boy, and the medicine man, too."

I didn't know if I liked being called boy, but it could be worse. "Thank you kindly," I said, and was about to nudge my roan out when he stopped me with a raised hand.

"Where'd ya get the roan?"

"The medicine man here stole him from the Crow."

"Better smear manure over that brand 'til you can re-work it." (Manure sticks longer than mud.)

"What's wrong with the brand?"

"You've been living with the Injuns too long, boy. That's a government brand, so unless you're on government business, you'd best have a bill of sale in your pocket."

It was something I hadn't considered, but I immediately dismounted and covered the brand with manure.

"I'd say off-hand," a second mountain man spoke up as I was remounting, "that it'd be easier to slip Charlie Jones a jug o' whisky for a forged bill o' sale than to alter the brand."

"Who's Charlie Jones?" I asked.

"He's the local drunk, when he can get a jug. Right now he's sleeping off a drink behind the corral." He threw a thumb over his shoulder, indicating where Charlie was sleeping.

"Where do I get the jug of whisky?"

"You sure don't know much, boy," the first man said. "You get the whisky where you sell the pelts."

I nodded, realizing that I indeed didn't know much. But before Uncle and I continued down the street, we rode around the corral to have a look at Charlie Jones, so that we would know him when we saw him in the light of sober-hood.

Lying in a mixture of dust and powdered manure, Charlie's

only source of protection from the Missouri sun was the shade of a single corral post. Red-faced and snoring, his appearance brought me up short. I had seen that face before, and would never forget it.

Charlie Jones had been a mobster! He had held the torch while the others were looting, but that was enough. Maybe he had set fire to the buildings, maybe not . . . who knows? Though his face had been blackened, the light of the torch had been full on his face that awful December night in 1838; the scene was burned forever into my memory.

A horsefly buzzed Charlie, undisturbed by the drunk's loud snores and offensive body odor. I looked long and hard, maybe a mite bitterly, too. Still, he wasn't the torch-toting mobster of bygone years; he was just a drunk, lying in the manure.

I wheeled my roan, pointing his head down the street. Maybe I flipped manure from the roan's prancing hooves into Charlie's open mouth . . . I didn't know, nor did I care much.

RAZORS, REVOLVERS, AND THE BOOK

As WE RODE down the street, a lone horse was standing three-legged in front of a building labeled "Saloon." As I repeated the word in my mind, I realized I could still read, though thinking in English was difficult.

Someone was thumping on a tinny-sounding piano inside the saloon. On the shady side of the street, several loafers held down wicker chairs tilted precariously against the plank wall of a weather-beaten building.

A man wearing a dueling pistol stepped off the board sidewalk and crossed the street in front of us, but as we grew closer I could see it wasn't a dueling pistol. The curious weapon was mostly concealed in a leather holster.

At the end of the street was a low trading post flanked by an assortment of wagons, ranging from a huge Conestoga to a light black buggy with green wheels. Behind the trading post was a corral that enclosed a dozen horses and mules.

We pulled rein in front of the building, and eyed a tall man with a wedge-shaped face standing in the doorway. He wore black cloth trousers and a white linen shirt with faded red garters. He looked past us, eyeing the packs on our animals.

"Do you buy pelts?" I asked.

"Sure thing. I'm George Poulsen, proprietor. I pay top dollar, but I only buy the best."

"We only have the best to sell," I replied.

"Take 'em around back and spread 'em out on the porch," he directed. "I'll look 'em over and make you an offer."

I nodded, and we nudged our animals to the rear of the building. We swung our legs over and jumped off, and were in the act of spreading the pelts on a low, covered porch when Mr. Poulsen stepped out. A man who knew what he was looking for, he went right to work examining the pelts, sorting them as he went.

"I'll take the lot of 'em," he announced, "and pay you $135 in Spanish gold coin or $150 in trade . . . you choose."

I translated for Uncle, though we were unfamiliar with the value of money, then asked Mr. Poulsen, "Why the difference in price?"

"I can get Spanish coin overland from Santa Fe, or up the Mississippi and Missouri from New Orleans, but I can't get enough to meet currency needs. So I charge my customers ten percent if I have to pay them in coin."

"Do you also buy gold nuggets?"

"Yes, but you have to take the gold to the assay office two doors up the street, and have it appraised. Most of my customers prefer to sell their gold directly to the assay officer, who will pay you in scrip, good only in Independence. You can bring the scrip back to me and I'll honor it for goods, giving you change in Spanish coin, but I'll still charge ten percent on the change."

Uncle and I set about making our choices according to our mental shopping list, though there were many things new and curious to us. My eyes lingered on some curious pistols like I'd seen the man in the street wearing earlier. "What are these?" I asked.

Mr. Poulsen retrieved one and handed it to me for my inspection. "They're called revolvers," he explained, "and I can hardly keep them in stock. As you can see, they have a revolving cylinder that holds six shots. The hammer rotates the cylinder as you pull it back. You can fire the six shots as fast as you can pull back on the hammer. A gent named Samuel Colt patented them back in '36, then started traveling around the country in a wagon—selling 'em and calling himself Doctor Colt.

"Are they accurate?"

"They're accurate as a rifle up to fifty or a hundred paces, but mostly it's good for Indian shooting, off-hand, close-in shooting without sighting. Peace officers are starting to use 'em because they can have both hands free, yet they can draw the weapon almighty quick when need be, and either shoot off-hand or aim. It looks peaceable for a peace officer to handle a problem without a rifle in his hand."

I nodded. 'Course with my throwing knife I didn't need a revolver. Still, a revolver seemed much like having six throwing knives and a rifle all in one. As I thought, I assembled our selections on the counter, which included pots and cloth, needles and beads, a razor and shaving items, a Sharp .50 for Uncle, and a jug of whisky. I watched Poulsen make the tally.

"Still got five dollars coming," he said.

"Keep track of it. We may think of something else before we leave Independence," I said. He nodded.

"Another thing," I said. "Where can I find a Mormon?"

"I don't exactly know," he replied slowly and suspiciously. "You know they killed Joseph Smith, don't you?"

I just stood there speechless for a moment. "You mean the . . . the mob in Caldwell County killed him?

Poulsen cast me another suspicious glance. "Mormons haven't

been in Missouri for six years," he said. "The state militia drove 'em out, but next thing we knew they had settled in Illinois, starting a town called Nauvoo. It's said they set Joseph Smith up as a general, but last month a town militia, called the Carthage Grays, killed him. Rumors have it that the Mormons are murdering and plundering in Illinois, burning crops and homes, seeking revenge on those that killed their prophet."

"Mormons are murdering, burning, and plundering?" I questioned.

"That's what they say. They're a vengeful lot. Joe Smith sent his destroying angel, Porter Rockwell, all the way back to Missouri a few years ago to murder Governor Boggs, but Rockwell missed. 'Course Rockwell denied it, saying if he had shot at Governor Boggs, he wouldn't have missed. Strange one, that Rockwell. I half believe him."

I was disturbed, I surely was, yet I tried to keep calm.

"If it's information on the Mormons you want, you could check with David Whitmer, but he's way up in Clay County," Poulsen offered. "Around here, I'd check with Jacob Foster; he's the local authority."

"Jacob Foster?" I questioned in disbelief. "He . . . he's a mobster!"

Poulsen eyed me suspiciously. "He helped drive the Mormons out of Caldwell county, I'll grant you that. But he was part of the state militia."

"He murdered my parents," I spoke quietly, coldly, "drove my mother out of her sickbed in the dead of winter. I saw him myself, and heard Mama call him by name. Then he gut-shot my Pa."

"Y . . . you a Mormon?"

"Uh-huh. I'm a Mormon, at least I was a Mormon. I don't know what I am, now."

"If you're a Mormon, I can't sell you the rifle, neither you nor the Indian."

"What do you mean?"

"In this part of Missouri, you can't sell rifles to either Mormons or Indians."

"Don't matter," I said, picking up the rifle with my left hand, my right hand hovering near my neck, close to my throwing knife. "You done sold it before you knew I was a Mormon, and as far as you're concerned, you still don't know."

"You'd best go, mister," Poulsen said. "I don't want trouble, and you sound like trouble."

I started to translate for Uncle, but was taken aback when he said in Pawnee, "I understood most of what he said. I haven't been your trainer for six years without learning a few words in English, though I would do better if he wouldn't speak so fast and slur his words." I nodded, watching Poulsen, as I didn't know how much I could trust him, while Uncle carried our purchases to our pack animals.

"Mister," Poulsen called as I was backing from the store.

"The name's Knife Thrower or Samuel Harold," I said. "You choose."

"Okay, Knife." He slapped what I later learned was a five-dollar value coin on the counter. "This is your change. You've done your business, so it's time for you to git. But if you come by another load of pelts like you just sold me, bring 'em to me and I'll buy them. I can't sell you or your Indian friend guns, but I'll sell you anything else."

I nodded.

"One thing more," he said. "I have something I think you can use." I hesitated, wary of him as he rummaged under the counter. It was a full minute until he came up with a book that looked curiously like a Book of Mormon. "Seeing you're a Mormon," he said, "you might appreciate this. A man traded it for food. A book is a book, and will usually sell regardless of what it is, so I made the trade."

"Then why don't you sell it?"

"Well, there has been this recent outbreak of Mormon hostilities, meaning no disrespect to you. It isn't safe to have their

101

Bible in stock, much less offer it for sale. So I tucked it under the counter, and was going to keep it hid 'til the Mormons quieted down."

I returned to the counter, pocketed the coin, and reverently picked up the book. "It's not a Bible," I said. "We Mormons use the same Bible as you do. It's writings of another people, an ancient people that lived on the American continent."

"Oh?" he questioned. "I didn't know that."

"Didn't you read any of it?"

"No. Foster claimed that to read it was to be blinded by the devil's spell."

"Mr. Poulsen," I said as I again backed out, "I'm only a lad of sixteen summers, but I can tell you that if you want to find out anything but hate about the Sioux, you shouldn't ask the Ojibway. Likewise, if you want to find out anything but hate about the Mormons, you shouldn't ask the mobsters."

CHARLIE JONES

U P THE STREET WE sold our gold nuggets and received $80 cash money. The coins were pretty, and I hoped they'd prove useful. If nothing else, Grandmother would likely take a shine to 'em.

As we passed the public corral on our way out of town, I noticed Charlie Jones sitting up, though in the same general spot where we had seen him earlier. "Let's circle the corral and speak with Charlie," I suggested. Uncle nodded and turned his mount, aiming for Charlie.

As we approached, Charlie appraised us through tired eyes. He touched his tongue to dry lips, then rubbed his face.

"You Charlie Jones?" I asked. 'Course I knew.

"Yeah," he replied. "That's what folks call me when they want somethin' from me." Powdered manure still clung to his hair and left ear. Again he touched his dry lips with an equally dry tongue.

I slung my leg over my Pawnee saddle and slipped to the ground, retrieving the jug of whisky. "Want a swallow of whisky to wet your whistle?" I asked.

"Uh-huh," he said, eyeing me suspiciously. He took a long pull of whisky that would have been longer had I not grabbed the jug away from him. Recapping it, I handed him a piece of jerky to chew.

"A fellow in buckskins suggested you'd create me a bill of sale for this here roan," I suggested.

"Yeah? I suppose he said all it'd cost you was a swallow of whisky?"

"No," I replied. "He said I should give you the whole jug."

"That's more like it," he replied. "What name do you want to use?"

"Samuel Harold," I said. Nearby was a stack of firewood. Walking to the wood, I retrieved a hunk of bark and scratched my name on its inner surface. "There's the name," I said as I plopped it in Charlie's lap. "Spell it right."

"Hain't nothing wrong with my spelling," he said as he picked up the bark. "I used to be a school teacher."

"Why aren't you still a school teacher?"

"I just seemed to lose the spirit of teaching five or six years ago, and started goin' downhill."

"You lost the spirit of teaching when you exchanged it for the spirit of hate against the Mormons," I suggested.

"What do you know 'bout that?" he demanded.

"Does the name 'Harold' sound familiar?"

"There used to be a family of Harolds up near Caldwell County." He eyed me suspiciously, but this time there was fear in his eyes.

"Same family," I replied.

"I had nothin' to do with it!" His voice was coming on good and strong, almost panicky.

"You held the torch!" I accused.

"God is my witness, that's all I did!"

"You stood by and let them turn my mother out of her sick-bed in the dead of winter, then watched as they tore down our cabin! You also watched them gut-shot my pa."

"Jacob Foster gut-shot your pa. Then he had to shoot him again in the forest so's he wouldn't spread the story to the few Missourians who were sympathetic to Mormons." He buried his face in his hands and sobbed, "I've been living with that for six years. When I went back to the schoolhouse, I couldn't teach after that . . . couldn't do anything but drink."

"Charlie," I said softly, "I didn't come here for revenge. I came here for a bill of sale because that roan means more to me than any horse alive."

"When do you want it?"

"When do you want the jug?"

"I'll have it ready tonight. I have a corner in the harness room, yonder. See you at sundown."

Finding a camping spot, we settled in as I read to Uncle from the Book of Mormon. I couldn't translate as I went, as I wasn't experienced, so I first read each sentence silently, then translated it aloud to Uncle.

I read through the testimonies of the witnesses, then began, "I Nephi, having been born of goodly parents, therefore I was taught somewhat in all the learning of my father . . .." As I began to repeat the sentence in Pawnee, I realized that I was a little like Nephi, as I had been taught by a "goodly" uncle.

Near sunset, we returned to Independence and made our way to the harness room where Charlie had his corner. He was waiting for us, red-faced with bloodshot eyes. "Here's your bill of sale," he said, slapping it in my right hand as he eyed the whisky jug I carried in my left hand. I looked it over, noting that it looked official, though what did I know? "Wrap it in a piece of oilcloth and keep it with you as long as the horse is young enough that a soldier or a government agent might want to lay claim to him," he advised. "One way to always have it with you is to stitch it inside your saddle."

"Indian saddles don't have stitching," I replied. "Fact is, they're hardly saddles."

"There are plenty of saddles for sale right here," he offered. "Mr. McCeary, the owner, buys 'em for little or nothing from western-bound immigrants who want to lighten their load, and sells 'em for $10 each. You can't hardly have one made for that price." He was still eyeing the whisky jug, so I handed it to him as I translated his words for Uncle.

Saddles are one of the paleface specialties that Indians have never perfected. Maybe it's because Indians haven't owned horses many generations, who knows? Saddles require a quality of tanned leather few tribes have mastered, and it takes heavy steel needles and awls to stitch the heavy leather, as bone needles aren't durable enough. So it didn't take Uncle and me any time at all to decide to part with one of our twenty-dollar gold pieces for two saddles, which Charlie helped us pick.

Stripping the Pawnee saddle from my roan, I threw one of the new saddles on his back, but was met with a string of curses from Charlie, who was standing directly behind me. "That's no way to treat a horse," he shouted. "Haven't you ever saddled a horse before?"

"Not with a leather saddle," I admitted. "When I was a boy, the horse was too high for me to saddle."

"I'll teach ya," he snapped. I stepped back as he proceeded to saddle the animal, explaining why he did what he did. The saddle blanket had to be almighty smooth, and positioned so it wouldn't roll. The rider's weight needed to be forward, but not too far forward, as you didn't want the rider's toes to interfere with the movement of the animal's front legs. The girth couldn't be too loose or too tight. Charlie talked to the horse as an Indian might, fussing over the animal like a child. I was impressed.

"Maybe you should quit drinking and go back to teaching," I said when he was finished. He looked embarrassed.

"Too late. I've done made my bed," he muttered.

I shrugged. "You got a razor?"

His face clouded. "Sure I got a razor. What's it to you?" He rubbed his facial stubble.

"I need someone to teach me how to shave, and it appears that you can use the practice."

"Everyone knows how to shave. You funning me, boy?"

"Everyone knows how to saddle a horse, too, but evidently there are some tricks." 'Course I'd seen Papa shave plenty, but that was years ago. Next time I stood before White Rabbit I didn't want to have blood dripping from my chin.

"Okay," he agreed. "Let's heat some water."

"Tell me about Jacob Foster," I asked as we waited for the water to heat.

"You don't want anything to do with him!"

"Why not? I'm not afraid."

"You ought to be," he replied. "Jacob is poison mean, though he has a glib tongue. He's got one of those revolvers and can hit anything he shoots at on the second shot, without sighting, providing he can see where his first shot goes. He counts himself high and mighty, a real bad man with a revolver. His hatred is fierce."

"Why does he hate Mormons so much?"

"Oh, it's not the Mormons that drives his hatred. He hates Indians."

"Indians? Why?"

"The usual thing; his parents were killed by a tribe of the Iroquois League, the Senecas or Mohawks, I don't know which. He hates the Mormons 'cuz Mormons are Indian lovers, or so it seems. Meaning no disrespect, but you'll notice you're traveling with an Indian."

"But Uncle is my family. My parents were killed by Missouri mobsters, but I don't hold all whites responsible, just Jacob Foster and his cronies."

He shifted uneasily. "Well, Jacob Foster hates more intensely than most men. He hates with a vengeance, and he loves hating. Indians, Mormons, negroes, Irishman, northerners, anything . . . Jacob hates 'em all. He especially hates people from Illinois."

"Why Illinois?"

"They're a high and mighty lot in Illinois, thinking themselves better than us. They call Missourians 'Pukes.'"

"I haven't seen Foster around town, though admittedly I haven't seen much."

"You'll recognize him when you see him, 'cuz he wears a black derby hat with a snakeskin band, though he says the band isn't snakeskin but hide peeled off Mormons, which he tanned. Still, he's not in town, but has gone west, saying he was hunting Injuns."

"What do you mean, 'hunting Injuns?'"

"I don't rightly know what he has in mind, but he says the only good Injuns are dead Injuns."

I cringed.

A BOYHOOD CABIN
AND A TESTIMONY

WITH THE SUMMER WIND in our faces, we rode a day's ride north, across the Missouri River to the remains of the home of my youth. It was a warm Missouri day, too warm for leather clothes. If I was going to dress in white man's clothes very much, I'd have to invest in some broadcloth trousers and a linen shirt.

Overhead a raven cried, and was answered by a second. Heat waves danced in the humid air, and now and again insects buzzed past. Part grassland, part clumps of forest, the landscape offered a variety of scenery.

The leather saddle was plumb comfortable, though it added extra weight. It was much easier to swing into a saddle using a leather stirrup than to bounce aboard. Glancing at Uncle, I was sure he was enjoying his saddle as much as I was enjoying mine.

We passed many small farms that smacked of nostalgia. Pigs wandered freely in small orchards and around homes, as pigs are the southerner's way of controlling snakes, and most local Missourians came from the south. They weren't slave-holding southerners, but only because slaves were too expensive for them. Still, they believed in slavery, and one of their gripes against the Mormons was that we were mostly northerners, labeled abolitionists by southerners.

Chickens roamed in the barnyards, but the chickens were generally kept separated from the pigs, as pigs liked to munch down on chickens that got in their way. When I was a lad, dogs and cats were scarce, but now everyone seemed to have 'em.

It wasn't easy for me to find the old cabin site. When I finally located it, it didn't seem exactly where I had remembered. Nothing was left but a few fireplace stones and footings; maybe the logs had been carted off for building materials for other cabins. It looked so small, not at all like the roomy cabin I had remembered. We swung down, and Uncle waited patiently as I looked around . . . remembering.

Overhead I heard the cry of a lone raven. Maybe it was the same raven I'd heard earlier in the day, who knows? Squirrels chattered, scolding each other. The hot late-afternoon sun scorched down, and beads of perspiration ran down the inside of my leather shirt. Enough of this, I thought as I whipped off the leather garment. Making my way back to my roan, I tied the shirt behind my saddle with my Hudson Bay blanket.

As I tied the shirt in place, I imagined my mother's voice saying, "Sammy, put on your shirt! Do you want to look like an Indian?" I glanced around, but I was alone save for Uncle, who was curiously studying me. I lowered my eyes, as my feelings were too personal to share, even with Uncle.

As a child I guess I was always a mother's boy, though I loved Papa, too. There was that special way she drew me to her and lifted my chin as she murmured, "You're like David of old, stalwart and dependable, and highly favored of the Lord." Maybe I was, maybe I wasn't, I surely didn't know; but I cherished her faith in me.

Mama had her special way of using her apron as a hot pad when lifting the cast-iron pot from the fireplace. "Don't do that," Papa repeatedly scolded. "One of these days you'll catch your apron on fire." So Mama would use her hot pad for a few days, but eventually she'd get in a hurry and use her apron again. 'Course she didn't have far to move the pot, as she always set it on the same hearth stone, the one that made the hollow sound.

I had already mounted to leave, but on an impulse I swung my leg across the saddle and jumped down, forgetting that the saddle was a durable leather saddle and all I had to do was swing down. Uncle cast me a curious glance but said nothing, as it wasn't his way to ask many questions.

Making my way to the rubble that had once been the fireplace, I cleared the stones down to the hearth, then tapped on the stones with a rock. One was hollow.

With a stick I started scratching out the stones without much success. In desperation I started from the outside and worked my way in, removing all the stones.

Underneath the hollow stone was a cedar box, rough-hewn but solid. A link to the past, it contained treasures from my parents' youth. There were scraps of material, maybe from a cherished girlhood dress, a slingshot, several war medals, a handful of tarnished silver coins, and a wedding ring. I knew the ring, as Mama had worn it a time or two. It had been passed down as a family heirloom. Some women had taken to always wearing their wedding rings, but that didn't used to be the case according to Mama.

For the second time we swung into the leather. Before we had gone far, I asked, "Do we have time to visit David Whitmer, Uncle? Mr. Poulsen, the storekeeper, said he lived in Clay County."

"You mean the witness whose testimony you read to me?"

"Ho."

"I thought you said he was excommunicated from the Mormons."

"He was . . . several months before the mob drove us out. Maybe he no longer holds to his testimony; I have to know."

"Why was he excommunicated?"

"I don't know. I was just a kid, and our family wasn't close to him."

"Do you know how to find his lodge?"

"We'll just ask."

The next day we rode up to the house that belonged to David Whitmer. A woman was sliding wood under a cast-iron washing kettle in the side yard. "Is this where David Whitmer lives?" I asked.

"Yes," she replied, eyeing us suspiciously. "Swing down and tie your mounts to the fence. He'll be here directly. He's gone to the house for a bar of soap." It surprised both Uncle and me that a man would be helping with the washing, as there was always so much man's work to be done that most men left the women's work to the ladies.

We swung down and loosened the cinches on our saddles, the way Charlie Jones had taught us. Minutes later, Whitmer appeared from the house with a bar of lye soap and a knife. The knife, of course, was for shaving the soap into the wash water.

"These gentlemen were asking about you, David," Mrs. Whitmer announced as her husband drew near. Depositing the soap and knife near the wash kettle, Whitmer approached, extending the right hand of fellowship.

"I'm David Whitmer."

"I'm Samuel Harold," I replied, accepting his hand, "and this is my friend Shunk." I felt a little shaky-kneed, knowing I was in the presence of one of the three witnesses.

"Used to know a Samuel Harold that lived next to the Caldwell County line."

"That was my pa."

"I liked your pa, though he seemed a might quick to condemn the gentiles." I scowled, but said nothing. "Haven't heard of him since the extermination order, but I suppose he moved to Nauvoo with the rest of the Mormons."

"No. He and my ma were killed by the mob. Papa was gut-shot by Jacob Foster, and Mama was turned out of her sickbed to die in the winter cold."

"Sorry to hear that, son. You say Jacob Foster shot your pa? Are you sure?"

"Sure I'm sure. Saw it myself. He used an old flintlock rifle that threw sparks."

"Don't say that too loudly around here. Jacob struts around with his revolver, cutting a wide swath." Then, eyeing Uncle, he asked, "Who did you say the Lamanite was?"

"He's my adoptive uncle. After my ma and pa were murdered, Shunk found me in the Indian Territories."

"That's a long way from here."

"Uh-huh," I replied.

I had a purpose in calling upon David Whitmer: I wanted to hear his testimony. This seemed as good a time as any to lead into it. "Does Shunk, being a Lamanite, look anything like Moroni?" I asked. It was said that David Whitmer and others were greeted by Moroni as they were traveling to the Whitmer farm to complete the translation of the Book of Mormon.

"No," he slowly replied. "Moroni was five feet eight or nine inches tall and heavy-set. His face was large and his hair and beard were white, though his beard was thin."

"Then you did see Moroni?"

"Yes, I saw him, as did Joseph, Emma, and Oliver. We were all in the wagon together."

"And did you actually see the angel and the gold plates?"

"I saw them as clearly as I see you and the Indian now. My testimony, as printed in the Book of Mormon, is true." The hair on the back of my neck seemed to stand on end as he looked into my eyes. For the next ten minutes he rehearsed the details of seeing the angel and handling the plates.

"W . . . why did you leave the Church?" I questioned, hesitant to ask, but curious.

"I didn't leave the Church, the high council kicked me out, though they didn't have authority to do so."

"Why did they kick you out?"

"Oh, the Word of Wisdom for one thing, but everyone knows the Word of Wisdom is just a suggestion. But that wasn't all. Joseph Smith wasn't perfect, you know. I was kicked out for telling the truth. I just pointed out some of his errors, told the truth, and they kicked me out." There was a touch of bitterness in his voice.

"But the Book of Mormon is true?" I asked.

"Yes, it is. The angel who showed the plates to us said it was translated by the gift and power of God. When he translated it, Joseph used two brown stones the shape of eggs, called the Urim and Thummim. It's all true . . . my testimony of the Book of Mormon will never change."

After a few more minutes of conversation, Uncle and I took our leave. We rode in silence for quite a while. Meeting one of the three witnesses and hearing his story had given us both a lot to think about.

WHITE RABBIT

A MULE BRAYED as we eased our mounts past the farm on the Missouri Platte, where six years earlier I'd stolen the leaky boat. The grass was heavy with dew that sparkled in the morning sunlight. A hen cackled, boasting of her accomplishments, and a cow mooed, calling the farmer to his milking.

The trail we were on was just a two-rutter, much of it overgrown with rye grass. It followed the Platte after a fashion, passing through occasional farmyards. In the stretches of scrub and hardwood forests between farms, the birds set up a feathered symphony the likes of which you never heard out on the prairie.

Two miles below the farm, we found a pile of deadfall seemingly waiting for us to come along and lash it into a raft, which we did. The pack animals could probably swim across with their loads lashed to their backs, but the river was strong and the packs heavy, making a raft a better idea. We had also grown attached to our saddles, but when leather gets wet, it's wet a long time, and we didn't want to spend the rest of the day sitting on wet saddles.

"I thought the cast-iron pots we purchased were large when we were in Independence," Uncle muttered as we loaded our raft, "but on seeing the huge cast-iron pots in some farmyards, ours don't stack up." I nodded. Some farmers had cast-iron tubs in their farmyards that were large enough to dip half a pig in for scalding and scraping. We had seen Mrs. Whitmer using such a pot as a washtub. Most wash water was heated over an open fire in the yard, but to have a pot as large as a wooden washtub amazed me.

As we crossed the Platte, Uncle led with the pack animals and my roan dragged the raft, as the big gelding was the strongest swimmer. When the Pawnee cross rivers, they don't usually use rafts, because along many rivers on the prairies there are only willows where the villagers want to cross. So they make buffalo-skin boats, using willows for the ribs. Then they pile their perishables and infants in the round-bottom boats and swim the boats across. For real rough rivers, sometimes parents will make an ark out of a buffalo-skin boat. We made a raft only because the logs were convenient and at hand.

The next day we crossed the Missouri River. Again we made a raft, but the river was so large that we stabilized the raft upstream with a guide rope tied around the neck of Uncle's calico.

A week later we rode into the village to the noise of barking dogs and jabbering children. While we were away the village had moved, and was now located a few hours away from Rice Lake on a small stream. Near the village the stream widened into a fair-sized swimming hole. In the six years I had lived with the Pawnee, we had camped at this site once every year, always in the summer, as it was located near Rice Lake for the rice harvest.

Blue Star ran to meet Uncle, who scooped her up like a child and sat her on his mount in front of him. Such carryings-on made me a little embarrassed, and I wondered how I'd be welcomed by White Rabbit.

When I swung down in front of Grandmother's lodge, Little Star was the first to emerge. At first she had eyes only for my leather saddle and wanted to try it out, flashing a hopeful glance in my direction. Only then did she notice my freshly-shaven face. She touched my smooth cheeks tenderly, smiling her approval. "White Rabbit will like that," she teased. Then she giggled as color started rising up my neck. Still, I was pleased that she had noticed. I helped her into my new saddle, then turned my attention to Grandmother.

"You did well," she grinned, studying my shave. "You look like a Pawnee now."

"Yes," I agreed, "but I have to heat water and shave every morning."

"Other white men get used to it," she said, cutting me no slack. "So will you."

"I also bought an object called a mirror so that I could see to shave, and I bought a second one for you." I dug into my pack and produced the mirror. Grandmother had seen mirrors before, but had never owned one. She seemed curious as she examined her face in the mirror, but I wasn't sure she was pleased, as mirrors don't lie.

Pick-a-Coal helped me unload my pack, and with curious neighbors looking on I exhibited my treasures to Grandmother. She was especially pleased with the steel knives and the cast-iron pot, though surprised at its weight. It was a round pot with a lid and three legs, something like a Dutch oven, though almost round, and held about two and a half gallons.

"It's an iron stomach," Grandmother observed.

"Almost," I replied. "My paleface mother had a pot just like it, and she used it for cooking the same way you use the stomachs of animals. The cast iron holds the heat, and the heavy lid makes it cook with pressure, so it cooks much faster than open cooking. But the cast iron takes special care, which I will teach you." Grandmother nodded, pleased. "I can make soup with it," she observed. (Only the old or sick Pawnee eat soup, as it's hard to make without pots.)

As is human nature, the neighbors too wanted cast-iron pots. But there was only one other in the village: the one Uncle had purchased for Blue Star, though it was a little smaller than Grandmother's.

Though a little young for courting, I had counted coup and earned an eagle feather, which made me eligible. So that evening

I sat by the trail to the stream, buffalo robe over my head, waiting for White Rabbit to make a trip for water.

I don't know how confident I looked, but I surely didn't feel confident. My mouth was dry and it was hot under the buffalo robe. What's worse, I was shaking, actually shaking.

Two maidens passed and giggled at me as I sat there waiting, peeping out through a tiny crack. It was a dumb way to court, really dumb, but it was proper. It was also a long wait; but eventually White Rabbit approached.

"Hello, beautiful maiden," I greeted as she eyed me curiously. It was the usual greeting of a boy courting a girl.

"Hello, Knife Thrower," she replied.

"How did you know it was me?" I asked, amazed.

"I know what your voice sounds like," she replied. In disgust I shook the robe off my head. It was too hot, anyway.

"Knife Thrower," she began, and the tone of her voice was too serious, "you . . . you're a good friend, the best boy friend I have, but Mother and Father say I don't want to court you. I'm too young to court without their permission."

"Why?" I asked as my whole life seemed to pass before my eyes. I couldn't be hearing what I was hearing, because without White Rabbit, life was empty and useless.

"For one thing, your face scrat . . ." She was about to say "scratches," making light of a situation she had little or no say in, but instead she stared at my clean-shaven face. "What did you do with your whiskers?" she asked.

"I shaved."

"But they're completely gone."

"No. Not completely. They'll be back tomorrow; it's the way of white men. Why won't your parents let me court you?"

"Because you're a white-eyes. My father's father was killed by a paleface, so he hated all white men until you came along. He likes you, but not enough to allow you to court me. If you ask, he'll be polite, but he'll tell you that you don't have enough horses to buy me."

She reached for my hand, gave it a squeeze, then hurried down the trail for her water without saying more. As I sat there I pulled the buffalo robe over my head, because Indians don't cry, yet my eyes were hot.

I guess I went back to Grandmother's lodge long-faced and pouting, though I tried to act passably chipper. Grandmother took me by the hand and led me to a secluded spot in the forest, where she pried the story out of me, as grandmothers do.

"There are other girls in the village besides White Rabbit," she counseled. "Meanwhile, we need fresh meat, as you have been away for many weeks. Why don't you go hunting?"

"I'll go," I replied as I straightened my shoulders. "I'll leave before dawn in the morning and catch the deer before they bed down."

That night I slept in the lodge of the warriors, or tried to. Sleep didn't come, so in the middle of the night I arose and made my way to the horse herd, saddle in hand. As I walked, I gave the proper signal to the sentries, which was the call of a quail. The roan nickered as I approached, and came to greet me. I patted his withers several times, then fussed over him as I saddled.

Five miles away was a salt lick, carefully stocked by Uncle and me; it was a favorite hunting spot. I approached from the down-wind side and dismounted, leaving my roan. Timing each step with the wave of the grass, I moved in. I was using a steel-tipped arrow, fresh from Poulsen's trading post in Independence, the first time I'd used such arrow tips.

To my disappointment, no deer were in the clearing, so I sat against the base of a tree and remained motionless. Presently two deer approached and looked directly at me. If you're down-wind from deer and remain perfectly still, they think you're a tree or something. As long as they have their heads up you remain frozen, but when they lower their heads you can move.

I waited until both deer had lowered their heads, then sighted on the nearest deer and let the arrow fly. Unlike buffalo, a deer will jump at the sound of an arrow and will usually bolt uphill, even with an arrow in its heart, and run for fifty feet or so. Uncle and I seldom off-hand shoot when we're using our hunting arrows, as one arrow is worth more than a deer. But the deer I shot bolted first, giving me a clear running shot at the second deer, and I took it.

As the village men were returning to their lodges from the Great Silence that morning, I walked into the village with two deer draped across my roan. White Rabbit had just stepped out of her lodge, and I could feel her eyes studying me as I passed.

Stopping in front of Grandmother's lodge, I was pleased when Grandmother stepped out, grinning. "You're as good a hunter as Shunk," she praised. I knew that wasn't exactly true, although, like Nephi's father, Uncle had taught me in all his learning.

I left the meat, then busied myself rubbing down my roan with handfuls of grass. There was a slight movement at my left elbow and I glanced over to see White Rabbit standing there, waiting to be noticed.

"Hello," she timidly greeted.

"Hello," I replied. "You walk quietly."

"You're not upset at me, are you?" Of course I was upset. Had she not rejected me?

"Oh, no," I replied, a bit sarcastically but with humor. "Why should I be upset, just because I missed a whole night's sleep because you broke my heart? As I was hunting last night I noticed that the moon no longer smiled because you rejected me, and I was surprised that the sun even rose this morning. Flowers have lost their scent, and the birds no longer sing to me—all because you rejected my pitiful efforts at courtship."

"All that because of me?" she grinned.

"All that and more," I replied. "But you didn't come by to hear that from me. What can I do for you?"

"I . . . I came by because I too noticed the flowers don't smell as sweetly without you." She cast me a coy expression. "I can't be courted by you, but still you're probably my best friend. Though," she added with a twinkle in her eye, "you could use a shave right now."

Uncle was approaching, so White Rabbit excused herself and returned to her lodge. "Will you come with Blue Star and me?" he asked. "We would like to vacation for a couple of weeks, until the rice harvest."

That would have seemed like an odd request to a paleface, because a paleface would expect a married couple to want to be alone for a mid-summer vacation. But it's dangerous for an Indian couple to vacation alone, so they usually have a tag-along riding ahead or behind for protection. A couple riding together is the same as a lone rider, and a lone rider isn't safe, although with Uncle's medicine marking on his pony he'd probably be safe.

"Ho," I replied. Being a tag-along wasn't something I relished, yet I'd do most anything for Uncle.

SMALLPOX

BLUE STAR'S EXCITEMENT was contagious as we moved out immediately following the Great Silence. I served as scout, riding ahead of Uncle and Blue Star, and was guided by prearranged animal calls: one call for left, two for right, three for distress . . . the usual thing.

I don't know that they had any specific destination, at least they had none that I could detect. We just wandered over hunting grounds familiar to both Uncle and me. Gathering herbs caught Blue Star's attention, and was as good an activity as any other. So for two weeks we gathered herbs, swam, feasted on the plentiful small game, and vacationed.

The nights were beginning to cool when we started for home, knowing the wild rice harvest was near. High, thin clouds covered the summer sun, providing a delightfully cool summer ride. We had traveled almost a complete circle, leaving the village riding north and returning from the south.

Leading Uncle by an eighth of a mile as we made our way through a scrub forest, I had been listening to a blue jay chatter when I heard the obnoxious jingle of a wagon. After giving the alarm to Uncle, I blended into the trees, stalking the jingle much as I would stalk prey.

It was a lone wagon pulled by two mules, and was bouncing as if it was empty. Flanking the wagon were two riders who seemed unconcerned for their personal safety. They must be pilgrims, I thought.

As they drew closer to where I was concealed, I noticed that the far rider wore a derby hat and carried a revolver on his right hip. Between his teeth was the stub of a cigar.

Jacob Foster!

I'd know the man who killed my pa even without Charlie's detailed description, and there he was, big as life. He hadn't changed, 'cept maybe he was a bit smaller than I had remembered, and his face was even harder. I fit an arrow to my bow, sighting on him. Maybe I should have counted coup right then; but I hesitated, as my mission was to provide safety for Uncle and Blue Star, not to get into a pitch battle with three no-account whites.

All evidence indicated that Foster and his henchmen were returning from our village, possibly from a trading expedition. Yet that didn't sound like what little I knew about the man. The bouncing wagon signaled that he hadn't traded for much, except maybe scattered gold nuggets kept by occasional villagers for their value with white traders.

When Foster and the wagon had passed, Uncle and Blue Star made their way to me for a parley. "They must have been coming from our village," I observed. "How many days' wagon travel would you say we are from the village?"

"Don't know," he replied. "You've seen a lot more wagons than I, even ridden in them. They don't move any faster along the Oregon trail than their milk cows walk, though this group was moving as fast as a walking horse."

I nodded in agreement. "That would mean they left our village four or five days ago."

"I don't like the looks of it," Uncle noted. "No one said anything about Foster being a trader."

When we were within a day's ride of the village, it was our

custom to pause to hunt, as we seldom entered the village empty-handed. Killing a blunt horn buffalo cow, we lashed the carcass to a travois and headed for the village.

Very few children were playing as we approached, and the usual hustle and bustle of a Pawnee village seemed subdued. Curious, we stopped a maiden who was walking for water. Uncle asked, "What's wrong in the village?"

"Paleface disease," she replied. "Three paleface devils rode in with blankets to trade a week ago. They didn't want much for the blankets, only gold nuggets. If a family didn't have nuggets, they were given a blanket anyway. The medicine men said the blankets contained the disease."

"What is the disease?" I asked. "Describe it to me."

"Those with the disease get hot with fever, then they get tiny sores that itch."

"Smallpox," I muttered as the maiden proceeded down to the stream.

"I have heard of it," Uncle said, "though I haven't seen it. Tell me what you know about it, Knife Thrower."

"There was an epidemic when I had seen seven summers. Those with the disease were not allowed to mingle with the rest of the community. It was summer, and the children swam a lot to keep down their fever, but they swam in a separate swimming hole. Mostly those with the pox were too weak to do anything 'cept eat and go to the privy.

"Papa assigned me to chop firewood for one family with smallpox. I threw the chopped firewood on their back porch, but I wasn't allowed to touch the porch."

"They say it's a killer."

"Yes. More than half of white people who get smallpox live, but it is said that Indians usually die. Papa said that when white people first came to New England, the Indians accidentally contracted smallpox from the whites and were nearly wiped out. Then the whites just moved in and took their land. Some church-goers say it was an act of God, but I don't know. It for sure eliminated some bloody wars with the whites."

"Maybe Foster is trying to play God and infected the Indians on purpose," Uncle observed.

"That's the way it looks."

"How do we protect ourselves?"

"I'm not real sure, Uncle. I was only seven when we had the epidemic. All I know is that the sick have to be isolated, and when someone dies their lodges should not be touched, but burned."

"Do palefaces burn the lodges of those who die?"

"No, not usually. They burn the outbuilding, clothes, and blankets, and sometimes destroy the family pet. Many whites are immune to smallpox, as they say once you've had it, you become immune. So someone who is immune cleans the home, burns what needs to be burned, and whitewashes the walls with a lime and salt mixture. There are probably many other ways to destroy the smallpox that I don't know, although they obviously don't all work, because we still have smallpox."

By then we had reached the lodge of Blue Star's mother. We stopped and Uncle swung down, as it is customary to always leave meat at your mother-in-law's lodge. The old lady stepped out, and we could see pox in her hairline and on her neck.

"Mother!" Blue Star screamed. She jumped to the ground and started for her mother. Equally fast, Uncle stepped between them. "You won't help your mother by getting the disease yourself!" he snapped.

"Go away," her mother ordered. "If you stay you might get the disease. Although," she added as she eyed the buffalo carcass, "fresh meat will be nice."

"I can't go," Blue Star protested. "You need me, and it's my duty to take care of you."

"We may need you," her mother replied, "but we would rather you go where it is safe so that you can raise our grandchildren."

"Where is it safe?"

Turning to Uncle, the old lady directed, "Take Blue Star to the Sioux village where you were raised. Return for the fall buffalo hunt."

"That is good counsel," a voice spoke from the rear. We turned to see Grandmother. She, too, had the pox. She was such a pitiful sight that I leaped to the ground and went to her. She backed off, protesting, "Don't touch me, Knife Thrower!"

"I was around smallpox when I had seven summers, Grandmother. There is a good chance I'm immune. If not, it doesn't matter, because I would just as soon die with the village."

"You must not die! If you die, there would be no one to avenge our deaths."

"Maybe you're immune, maybe you're not," Uncle reasoned, looking me in the eye. "Still, from what you told me, you should avoid direct contact with the sick, as you might carry the disease on your clothes to others. Stay with Blue Star and me in our lodge, and we, all three of us, will busy ourselves hunting meat and gathering firewood for the sick."

"That is a good plan," Grandmother said weakly. "There are many sick, and most of them are too weak to hunt."

In my concern over Grandmother, I had forgotten about my sisters, but now I remembered them. "Are Little Star and Pick-a-Coal free of the sickness?" I asked.

"No," Grandmother replied. "They are sick, too."

We led our mounts to Uncle's lodge, where Blue Star divided the buffalo carcass into small packages of meat, then sent me as a runner to deliver the meat to those in need. One lodge I delivered meat to was the lodge of White Rabbit. As she stepped to the door after I had hailed the lodge, I was glad to see that she didn't have any visible pox. Still, she seemed tired.

"Do you have the smallpox in your lodge, White Rabbit?" I asked.

"Is that what it is called?" she replied.

"That's what palefaces call it."

"None of us have the pox, but I am tired, and I have a fever."

"You . . . you must not have it, White Rabbit!"

"Why?"

"Because I . . . I love you," I said softly.

"I love you too, Knife Thrower. These weeks you have been gone seemed like forever."

The next week was spent hunting, and every day we returned to the village to share our kill with the needy. Blue Star stayed with us, because Uncle wanted to keep her from the temptation of visiting the sick in the village.

Every day, we heard the death chants as we rode in. The cold hatred began brewing anew in my soul for the man responsible, Jacob Foster. I didn't like to feel myself hating, yet I couldn't help it, and I promised myself I would avenge these deaths. I would kill Jacob Foster, which was the Indian way.

I had taken to keeping the Book of Mormon in my saddle bag. Every day I would read to Uncle and Blue Star from it. Still, I couldn't shake the hatred in my soul.

One day as we were butchering our kill, a man approached on foot, which seemed odd. To my surprise I saw that he was a white man, yet he seemed to have the features of an Indian. Uncle seemed to know him, and suddenly I suspected he was one of the three Nephite prophets.

"Greetings," Uncle said.

"Greetings," he replied. "That is a fine buffalo. The people in your village will appreciate the meat."

"Yes," Uncle agreed. "There is much suffering and death in our village. The sick need the meat, as they are too weak to hunt for themselves."

"You do well to feed those who are sick and mourning, but your heart is sad, as are the hearts of Blue Star and Knife Thrower." As he spoke he looked into the eyes of Blue Star, then into mine, and he seemed to be looking into my soul. I could feel the peace of the Nephite's spirit as a warm glow of love spread through my being.

"If God wills to take your whole village unto himself," he said, returning his gaze to Uncle, "so be it. Still, there are many wicked who need time to repent and learn patience, so God will cut short the sickness."

"You mean," I said in amazement, "that God will save the village because of the wicked ones?"

"All men have wickedness," he replied slowly . . . teaching. "Were it not so, they would be translated. Do you not recall in the Book of Commandments, Martin Harris was called a wicked man?"

"Yes, I recall," I replied.

"All mankind are the sons and daughters of God, and deserve time to repent of their sins. The wicked need more time than the righteous, as they have more repenting to do. You have some repenting to do, too, Knife Thrower. Your heart is hard, burdened down with thoughts of vengeance."

I squirmed a little. Obviously the Nephite knew all my sins—sins I intended to forsake. "What would you have me do?" I said, willing to follow anything he counseled.

"Do you want your own revenge against Jacob Foster, or God's vengeance? You can't have both."

"God's vengeance," I said, seeing my sins in a new light.

"You spoke well, because 'vengeance is mine, saith the Lord.' God wants you to be a great warrior, but warriors can only be great in the sight of God if they fight for the right reason. Do you think General Moroni fought the Lamanites for vengeance, or to bring peace?"

"To bring peace."

"You have spoken well again, Knife Thrower. If you remember that and fight to bring peace rather than to seek revenge, you will be a great man in God's eyes and a peacemaker between the Lamanites and the gentiles. The two cultures must learn to live in peace. The Lamanites have had this land for fourteen hundred years, but now they must share it."

"This is the Indian's hunting ground and will always be so, won't it?" I questioned. "White men can't possibly live here, because the great herds of buffalo would push over their fences and trample their farms," I observed.

"If it is God's will to sweep this land free of the great herds, he will do it. God is the gardener of this vineyard, and he will dress it as he sees fit."

That afternoon as we made our way into the village, Pick-a-Coal met us. On her face and in her hair were ashes, so I knew the answer before I asked.

"Grandmother has died?" I asked.

"Yes," she replied. "She said you were to avenge her death."

"I will do as the Great Spirit directs, whatever it is," I promised.

I took my sister in my arms, and could feel the great sobs of grief from inside her. I just held her, and suddenly I noticed that her pox were gone. "Pick-a-Coal," I said, "the Great Spirit has taken the sickness from your body!"

Surprised, she put her hand to her face and felt for the pox that weren't there. In spite of her mourning, a grin spread over her face. "I hadn't noticed," she admitted.

"My pox are gone, too," Little Star added in amazement. I hadn't realized she was there, at my left elbow. I drew her into our circle, and there we were, a family of three. But we wouldn't be a family of three for long, because Pick-a-Coal had been making concessions to one particular courter, a timid warrior named Black Buffalo. Black Buffalo hadn't counted coup, but Pick-a-Coal didn't seem to care; he was a good hunter.

"Knife Thrower," Pick-a-Coal said, "White Rabbit has been asking for you."

"I will go to her."

"Be careful."

"I think it is safe," I said. "I think I am immune to smallpox."

I made my way to White Rabbit's tepee and hailed the lodge. No one responded, so I hailed again. From inside came a weak voice. "Please enter, Knife Thrower."

Timidly I entered, and gave my eyes a few moments to grow accustomed to the diminished light. The smell of death was in the air, but only one person was in the lodge: White Rabbit.

"Where are your parents?" I asked.

"They died this morning," White Rabbit replied, tiny sobs shaking her body. I went to her and took her in my arms.

"You are now alone?" I asked.

"Yes," she replied. "I am alone, but I fear I am dying."

I just sat there holding her, fearful that her shallow breathing wouldn't continue. "Once," she began, "you courted me."

"I would court you again, if you would let me."

"Would you?" she asked, cocking her head to peer into my eyes.

"Yes," I replied.

"Would you ask me to marry you?"

"Yes. Would you accept?"

"I would accept."

"Then," I began, "White Rabbit, will you marry me?"

"Yes, though I fear death will take me first."

After half an hour, Pick-a-Coal joined us. It was getting dark, and throughout the night I held White Rabbit in my arms. Her breaths came shallow and ragged, then near morning they didn't come at all.

Pick-a-Coal took her from my arms. "I will prepare her body," she said. "It's time you go."

I went hunting, because I knew nothing else to do. For days I saw her in my dreams every time I closed my eyes. They say time heals everything, but there are some aches that time never fully heals.

THE PAWNEE BAND

THE SMALLPOX EPIDEMIC was over, or at least grinding down. More than half of our village was gone, but even at that we were better off than most villages I'd heard about. Those left in the village now had resistance to the smallpox. Under Uncle's direction, we burned the lodges of the dead.

Our rice harvest had come and gone during the sickness, and the crop would be sorely missed. Yet, thanks to the muskrat tribe, we had as many beans as other years, and only half as many villagers to share them.

As we sat in the council lodge one day, visiting and laughing as Indians do, the war chief, Snake Eyes, spoke on a serious note, saying, "We must consider uniting ourselves with another village, as we are now so small that we can't defend ourselves. Soon the Crow or Sioux will come, counting coup, and we will be easy prey."

"It is not safe for us to unite with another village yet," replied No Nose, the village chief. "We are now immune to smallpox, but we may still carry the evil on the walls of our lodges. If we unite with another village and they get the evil, we will be condemned."

"Is it better to be condemned, or be slaughtered by the Crow?" Snake Eyes snapped back.

"We can be as strong as we have ever been," Uncle interjected, "if we tell our young men to stay home from counting coup and defend the village."

"Our young men will not do that," said a respected old man. "If they do not count coup, they cannot court. If they do not court, they won't get married, and we will always be an oversized band of Pawnee rather than a village."

"It is good for our young men to prove their bravery, but counting coup is stupid," Uncle boldly replied. "I fear that by slaughtering other tribes we offend Ti-rá-wa."

"You speak like a coward!" declared Snake Eyes, grabbing his tomahawk. It was the first time in nearly a year I had heard someone call Uncle a coward. The air was suddenly tense, because Uncle was now a respected man who had counted coup. He was a medicine man, and was by far the most successful hunter in the village.

"If you come at me with that tomahawk, Snake Eyes," Uncle threatened, "you will die. That would be a shame, because your skill as a warrior will be needed when the Crow come counting coup."

Everyone was bewildered, even I. No one had ever heard Uncle challenge anyone, let alone Snake Eyes, the war chief. The situation was indeed serious, because without Uncle's hunting magic or Snake Eyes' fighting skills, our oversized band might be destroyed.

"You must appreciate, Snake Eyes," Uncle continued, "that for the past three autumns you have been away counting coup, and we have had to defend ourselves against the Crow without you. Someone else has had to defend your wife and children. If it were not for us at home in the village, your family would be dead, or Crow slaves. Are you proud of that?"

"I will kill you!" Snake Eyes screamed.

"No, you won't," spoke the war priest, almost in a whisper. All eyes turned to him.

"What did you say?" asked No Nose.

"In a mixture of badger and buffalo blood, I saw Shunktokecha's face." (A mixture of badger and buffalo blood is the usual concoction for medicine men to use as a medium to see the outcome of a raid.) "I do not know why Shunktokecha insults our sacred tradition of counting coup, nor do I know why Ti-rá-wa favors him over the rest of us medicine men," the war priest frankly stated.

As if on a prearranged signal, all eyes turned to Crooked Teeth, the chief medicine man and the wisest man in the village. There are many chiefs in most villages—a chief for everything important in a villager's life. Crooked Teeth no longer had teeth, but had to live on soup and soft food.

"It is true," Crooked Teeth said. "At the time of Knife Thrower's hanblechia, Shunktokecha had his medicine hanblechia. During their hanblechias it was my lot to watch over them, as in their weakened state they might fall prey to prowling animals.

"When I approached Shunktokecha's cave on his third morning of fasting, he was sitting by his fire conversing with someone. As candidates are supposed to be alone for their hanblechia, I was concerned. But as I watched, Shunktokecha and the stranger apparently completed their conversation, and the stranger vanished. He didn't walk away, he just instantly vanished.

"That evening, Shunktokecha and Knife Thrower saved our village from a Crow attack, performing marvelous feats that were unbelievable, yet they had the scalps and horses to prove it. The next morning we found the tracks where Shunktokecha had spoiled the attack of a large Crow war party." Crooked Teeth eyed the villagers and many nodded, as it was a well-known story.

"If Shunktokecha says our young men should stay home to protect our village," Crooked Teeth said, "we should follow his counsel." There was a chorus of agreement from the villagers. But the young men were clearly concerned, having been raised with the teaching that counting coup was evidence that they were warriors.

The great fall hunts came and went successfully; there was meat in every lodge, in various stages of curing. The women's work of tanning the many hides was in full swing, and the young men, who preferred to count coup rather than tan hides, were mourning their fate.

Camped on the prairie where the fall hunt took place, the main task of the young warriors was to erect the usual windbreak fence around the village. The high pole fence, which did duty as a fort, wasn't as hard to construct as one might have thought, as many poles were at hand from the last winter's pole fence.

A modest effort was made to make the village seem larger than it actually was, giving the appearance of greater strength. In many ways we were stronger than we had ever been, because we realized our weaknesses and were careful. The downfall of most villages seemed to be the result of sheer carelessness and complacency.

We were comparatively rich in horses, because the surviving villagers inherited the horses of those who were struck down by smallpox. But to be rich in anything that someone else wants is not always good. Much of our young men's time was spent on lonely guard duty, a task as dreary as tanning buffalo hides, leaving little time for courting.

Enemies might up and count coup anytime during the year, but certain times are more likely than others. All tribes have to hunt winter meat in the cool days of early fall, and they have to gather seeds and pick berries when the seeds are dropping and the berries are ripe. In the deep cold of winter, the same snows that restrict your travel protect you from your enemies. So late fall and early summer are the most likely times for enemy attacks. Of the two, late fall is the most dangerous, as there are fewer insects to give warning of prowling enemies.

The ponies had been divided into two herds for greater protection, and Black Buffalo had taken to bedding down with the north pony herd, as had other young warriors. They were using the ponies as watchdogs, as ponies can sense movement out in the prairie long before the sentries. Ponies are curious creatures, so they pay attention to movement.

Normally I didn't have sentry duties, as I had the duties of a village hunter. But I didn't share the Pawnee's superstitions over spirit movements in the night, so the night the Sioux came I was bedded down near my prospective brother-in-law, Black Buffalo, at the edge of the north herd.

I was awakened by the chirp of a cricket from Black Buffalo, the assigned distress signal for the night, and saw the ponies looking out into the prairie. The tribes close to us send out their scouts and maneuver into position at night, but they don't usually attack at night because of the possibility of having their spirits wander in darkness, should they be killed.

Several buffalo hump shields had been set up around the herd, hopefully to give impressions of sentry locations. In the vacant areas between the shields we had planted lariat booby traps. Lariats were used by the Indians long before cattlemen considered using them to lasso stray cattle, much for the same use. It was Uncle's idea to use lariat traps, as he had seen them used by the Sioux when he was a lad. According to Uncle, it was good psychological warfare to catch a scout alive and tie him to the village fence before the day of the attack, thus sending a message that the attackers were not favored by the gods.

In the starlight, I could see a wave in the grass moving toward one of our lariat traps between Black Buffalo and me. As the Crow had been attacking us recently, I could imagine an ugly Crow behind the waves, and I prayed he would slide into our trap.

The easy wave drew closer, and I was impressed at the enemy's skill in moving through close grass. Fact is, were it not for the close training Uncle gave me, I could not have detected a movement at all.

Suddenly the enemy sprang the trap, and Black Buffalo snapped back, drawing the noose tight. The enemy rose to his knees, and I saw the flash of his knife in the starlight as he lashed at the lariat. I threw my knife, not wanting the enemy to slice the lariat and escape. I didn't want to kill him, as we had other plans for him; but if he died, so be it.

I closed the distance between the enemy and myself as I drew my waist knife. One of his arms was pinned to his side by the lariat, and my throwing knife quivered in his shoulder. Yet he was game, holding his knife steady, ready to die like a warrior. Black Buffalo gave a quick snap of the rope, allowing me to kick the enemy's knife from his hand, then I doubled him up with a solid blow to his wind.

We didn't waste any time but bound him quickly, as he was clearly no pilgrim at fighting. Drawing my knife from his shoulder, I slapped on some herbs, as he wouldn't be useful to us if he bled to death. As I did so he spat in my face. "I spit on you because Pawnee are old women!" he jeered. It surprised me that I knew what he was saying; then I realized I understood some words because he was speaking in Sioux, and Uncle had taught me many Sioux words.

His reason for taunting us was not only to show bravery, but to possibly make us mad so that we would kill him quickly, thus he'd avoid torture. But as I wiped the spittle from my face, I thought of a way Uncle had taught me to throw the fear of God into a prisoner caught at night. "Would you take the squaw's tormenting in the light of day, or would you rather die quickly at night, your spirit wandering in the darkness?" He didn't respond, but I knew what he had in mind. He'd hold off jeering us until daylight.

By then a tight group of young warriors had gathered, anxious to get in on the action. We moved our prisoner to the village, the outside warriors using their shields to keep other enemy scouts from attempting shots.

When we reached the village fence, we tied ropes to our prisoner's arms and legs, then spread-eagled him against the pole fence, tying him securely. Then we built a fire in front of him so the enemy could see their scout. It would cause them to reconsider the backing they were receiving from the spirits.

"Tell me, warrior who thinks he is brave, why does a high Sioux warrior scout fall into a Sioux trap?" I asked.

"How did big mouth who is ugly as a buffalo know it was a Sioux trap?" he asked in reply. "Why do you know the pure language?"

"My uncle is a Sioux. He was captured as a boy."

"The Pawnee must not think very highly of you, or they wouldn't give you a Sioux as an uncle."

"I, too, am a captive," I replied. "But Uncle is a respected medicine man."

"What is your uncle's name?"

"Shunktokecha."

"Shunktokecha? There was a boy in our village who had that name when I was young, but he is no more. He died while I was away counting coup against the Ojibway. I would have your uncle see me before I die."

"What was your Shunktokecha like?"

"He was very strange. They say he talked with the animal tribe. His baby name was Shunktokecha, because he would sneak into his mother's buffalo robes like a coyote, and snuggle between his mother and father."

"What is your name? . . . in case Uncle knows you."

"I am Deer Tracker. The Shunktokecha I speak of was my brother."

DEER TRACKER

IF DEER TRACKER was indeed Uncle's brother, we needed to keep the Sioux from killing him . . . a mercy killing to keep him from being tortured. It was a fairly simple matter to keep an enemy from creeping close enough to use a bow and arrow, but some Indians had rifles.

The grass next to the fence had been burned, creating a fire line, but not the grass farther away, where a rifleman might crouch. Yet if we cut our prisoner from the fence before the Sioux advanced for the morning attack, they wouldn't see that we had him, so he would be of no value in deterring the attack.

It was still the middle of the night, but we made our way to war chief Snake Eyes' lodge and awakened him with three cricket chirps. He listened attentively as we explained the danger, then, still dressed in nothing but his clout, followed us to awaken Uncle. Responding to the three chirps of the cricket, Uncle emerged with his new rifle in hand, ready for war, and looked bewildered when he saw us standing there with Eagle Eyes.

"The young warriors have a prisoner tied to the fence," Eagle Eyes announced. Uncle grunted in satisfaction. "We will take you to him."

"Why should I go to him?" Uncle questioned.

"He is Sioux," I explained, "and says he used to know a lad named Shunktokecha."

Suddenly wide awake, we started for the village gate. "They say everyone in my village was killed or taken captive when I was taken captive, and I didn't know anyone from other villages," Uncle said.

"He says he was counting coup when you were captured. Does the name 'Deer Tracker' sound familiar?"

"Deer Tracker was my brother," Uncle said. He quickened his pace. "Who owns the prisoner?" A warrior who captured a prisoner owned him, so if someone else in the tribe wanted the prisoner, they had to negotiate with the owner.

"Black Buffalo and Knife Thrower own the prisoner," Eagle Eyes said, "but they have him tied on the outside of the fence as an exhibit, as you suggested."

Deer Tracker's head was bowed, his chin resting on his chest, when we approached. He looked up into the face of Uncle. Recognition filled his countenance.

"Shunktokecha," he said softly, "I thought I would never see your face again. Mother said you were dead."

"Mother?" Uncle questioned. "It can't be. She died when I was captured. I heard the Pawnee boasting that everyone was killed."

"When the raid came, everyone was not hidden in the same location. The Pawnee found only half the village. Your mother and sister are still alive."

"Knife Thrower said you were away counting coup. I had not remembered that."

"I was with the war party. If we had been home, the Pawnee would not have been victorious."

Turning to Eagle Eyes, Uncle announced, "He is my brother."

"Untie him," Eagle Eyes announced.

"Even if he is Uncle's brother," I put in, "don't we need him exhibited so that his war party knows we have captured him?"

"He's your prisoner, Knife Thrower, but he can tell his war party in person that we captured him, if you release him."

"What are you going to have him say to his war chief?" I asked, bewildered.

"It's always best," Snake Eyes said a little sarcastically, "if a scout tells his war chief the truth and describes everything exactly as he saw it."

"Very well," I said. "You're the war chief."

"I'm glad you recognize it; I was beginning to wonder," he replied. Then, turning to Uncle, Snake Eyes ordered, "See that Deer Tracker gets through our line, Shunktokecha. Give him a horse if he needs one."

"You're making it easy for him to get away," Uncle noted.

"That's right. Tell him to tell his war chief to be on time in the morning. Tell him Chief Snake Eyes and his braves don't want to waste too much time lifting Sioux scalps, because we want to be back to our lodges for breakfast." Uncle translated.

Snake Eyes started to leave, then paused long enough to spit on Deer Tracker the same way Deer Tracker had spit on me. "Does your war chief wear a dress?" he snapped.

Deer Tracker was cut loose, almost falling into Uncle's arms. For long moments the two brothers embraced, conversing in low tones. Of necessity the reunion had to be short.

"Tell Mother I shall hold her in my arms when the earth warms next summer," Uncle said.

"Ho," Deer Tracker replied. "I will tell her."

Uncle and Deer Tracker slipped into the pre-dawn darkness, leaving Black Buffalo and me standing by the fire outside the fence. Uncle, of course, was leading his brother through the sentry lines as Snake Eyes had ordered.

"Chief Snake Eyes knows how to talk tough," Black Buffalo muttered. "I wonder if the Sioux will attack in the morning."

"I don't know if Snake Eyes convinced Deer Tracker," I replied, "but he convinced me. If I were Deer Tracker's war chief, and I received Deer Tracker's honest report, I would sure as heck know my medicine had gone sour, even with giving Snake Eyes credit for being a bluff, though I'm not sure he was bluffing."

Morning came and we were ready, but the Sioux didn't attack. When the scouts went out, they saw the marking where the Sioux had been. The trail led north to the Sioux hunting grounds. After two weeks, heavy snows halted the yearly slaughter of counting coup. Still, Black Buffalo earned an eagle feather, as you don't have to kill an enemy to count coup—not if you have a witness.

The winter came cold and harsh, but there was food in every lodge. As usual we ran low on fuel, and many couples found it best to wed and cuddle together under the same buffalo robe. One of these couples was Pick-a-Coal and Black Buffalo.

Still, things were different. Uncle often looked to the north, to the land of the Sioux. "My mother is alive," he'd mutter. "In the spring I'm going home."

"This is your home," Blue Star would say.

"Home is where your family is," Uncle would inevitably reply. "I haven't seen Mother since I had twelve summers. I want to see her again, to look into her eyes, and to hear the chants of my childhood again before she grows too old and crosses the Great River."

JACOB FOSTER

SPRING CAME, bringing the celebration of the New Beginnings. Those who had died during the smallpox epidemic were nearly forgotten, or so it seemed. Yet I have one of those stubborn hearts that longs for those I love. Like I longed for Mama and Papa, I longed for Grandmother, that special person who thought I was something special. But I mentally blocked out White Rabbit, or tried to. Of course I believed in the eternity of the soul and knew that somewhere White Rabbit lived, but her death was painfully final, in an earthly sense.

I lived in the lodge of the warriors, and Little Star lived with Pick-a-Coal and Black Buffalo. Increasingly I was just there, a bachelor. Yet I was different from the other bachelors—not in the color of my skin, but in the color of my values. The nightly stories of counting coup from the other young warriors had lost their exciting edge, though I loved the retelling of the boyhood days when we made war on bees and explored the activities of the animal tribes. Increasingly I sat alone and reread the Book of Mormon, or spent days hunting and studying nature. Somewhere in the back of my mind, I wondered what happened to the Mormons after Joseph Smith died.

I came in from hunting one warm spring day to find Uncle and Blue Star striking their lodge. "I thought you were going to wait for the hot days of summer to search for your family," I protested.

"We were, but it's warm enough now. The ache to find my elderly mother and hold her in my arms is strong. Besides, we have the winter pelts to sell."

A lump formed in my throat. I, too, wanted to look into Mama's or Grandmother's eyes, and hold them in my arms. I didn't blame Uncle for searching out his family, as I would have done the same had I had a chance.

"Are you taking your lodge with you?"

"We're going to stash our lodge in the cache near Rice Lake. Come with us," Uncle said, catching me staring out into the prairie. "I will teach you the ways of the Sioux, as I've taught you the ways of the Pawnee."

"You've taught me the ways of the Sioux, Uncle . . . even taught me some of their language. I'll wait for you to get settled and become a big man in your Sioux tribe, then maybe I'll visit you. But right now," I said, returning my gaze to the waving grass of the prairie, "I think I've gotten a bad case of wanderlust."

Uncle nodded. "We both have many winter pelts to sell in Independence. Shall we travel together?"

I brightened. "I'd like that . . . just like last year when the three of us traveled around the hunting grounds together."

The newest generation of Pawnee were chasing gourds down a slope, the older boys were preparing to wage war on bees, and overhead a raven cried. Life in the village was as it should be as Uncle, Blue Star and I paused to take it all in, then turned our minds to our next stop, a cache near Rice Lake where Uncle would leave his lodge.

Leading a string of pack horses, it took us two days to reach the cache. There we strung the buffalo hides from Uncle's lodge high in the young trees. Not far away were other caches, some of them years old. They were safe from everything except varmints, though at times varmints have two legs.

Our load considerably lightened, we struck a course southeast to Poulsen's trading post in Independence. With a quickness born of purpose, we made good time in the pleasant spring days. Blue Star was especially excited over visiting a white settlement, as the magic and greed of the paleface was well exaggerated at storytelling times in all Pawnee lodges.

Catching the Santa Fe Trail near Westport Landing, we followed it into paleface country. Both thrilled and apprehensive over the wonders of the paleface farms and homes, Blue Star seemed to take it all in. A day later we cantered our mounts to the outskirts of Independence, a town so large it was frightening.

As we passed the corral where we had first seen Charlie Jones the year before, a half dozen men were again gathered, passing a jug and swapping stories. They glanced at us as we passed, their eyes lingering on Blue Star. It was my guess that Indian women were not often seen in the white settlements, so she was something of a novelty.

Apart from the others, seated in a wicker chair that was tilted precariously against the stable wall outside the harness room, Charlie Jones was snoozing, or trying to in spite of a pesky horsefly. On an impulse, Uncle pulled rein in front of him and bucked his mount to a stop, dust clouding higher than he anticipated.

Charlie coughed a little, making a feeble attempt to fan away the dust with his hand. "Ain't you got any respect for a man trying to catch a few winks in the middle of the morning?" he grumbled. Uncle grunted but said nothing more 'til Charlie gave him his full attention.

"You got another saddle, I buy?" Uncle spoke slowly in English.

Charlie studied Uncle in bewilderment for a moment, finally recognizing him. "Uh-huh," he said. "You got ten dollars?"

"Yes. I come back for saddle."

As Uncle started to rein around, Charlie added, "Rumor has

it that the Pawnee are on the warpath, if there are enough of 'em left after the smallpox epidemic."

"How did you know about the smallpox epidemic?" I asked.

"Jacob Foster is spreading stories of it around town."

"Jacob Foster would know," I said, "because he is one of three men who sold smallpox-infested blankets to the Indians."

Charlie looked shocked, then shrugged it off. "Don't say that too loud, someone might hear. Foster is already gunning for you, Samuel."

"Gunning for me? Why?"

"When you were here last summer you spread the word that he murdered your ma and pa. Folks around here don't like the Mormons, but they pretend they drove 'em out civilized like, rather than murdering 'em. Evidence of murder strikes a guilty cord."

"Jacob Foster murdered my parents, and that surely wasn't civilized! Then he infected an entire Pawnee village with smallpox-infested blankets! Tell folks that, ya hear?"

"I hear," he grinned, "but you better start running or toting a gun, 'cuz in a few days there won't be room enough in Independence for the both of you. He's so sick with a cough that he can hardly breathe. The only thing that gives him some measure of relief is his cigar, but all he can think of is killin' and vengeance. It's like he was possessed."

"Maybe he is," I replied as I reined my mount around and started down the street.

As we passed the saloon, a loafer with the stub of a cigar between his teeth stared at us. Noting his black derby hat, I threw him a sidelong glance. Then I glanced again.

It was Jacob Foster!

There was no recognition on his part, as I was a child when he last saw me. But as his gaze passed from me to Uncle and Blue Star, a smile spread over his lips. It wasn't a nice smile, either.

Not bothering to stop at the front door of Poulsen's store, we continued on around back where he had us lay out our pelts the year before. Uncle and I had swung down, and he was helping Blue Star down when Poulsen stepped out.

"Hope your pelts are of the same caliber as the ones last year," he barked, seeming a little grouchy. "I'll only take the best, you know."

"We know," I replied as we began untying the cords that bound the pelts. "Hope your trade items are as good as the trade items you had last year."

"They're just as good," he responded, eyeing Blue Star. "Who's the squaw?"

"She's the medicine man's wife . . . name is Blue Star." Turning to Blue Star, I said in Pawnee, "This is the paleface trader." Greetings were exchanged, then Poulsen went to examining the pelts.

One at a time, Poulsen went over every inch of the pelts. He evidently knew exactly what he was looking for and wasn't going to be stuck with less than perfect pelts, sorting them as he looked them over, the same as he had done the previous year. Then he carefully counted and recounted.

"One hundred ten in merchandise or ninety-nine in coin," he offered.

"One hundred twenty," Uncle responded for absolutely no reason 'cept that Indians insist on dickering. I was a little surprised, as it was the first time I'd heard Uncle use his limited English vocabulary for bartering.

Poulsen grinned, knowing what to expect. "One hundred fifteen, and that's final!"

"One hundred fifteen and three pieces hard candy, then final," Uncle replied. Poulsen chuckled and agreed.

"Is my share of the hundred fifteen dollars enough to buy one of those little pistols?" I asked.

"I can't sell guns to Mormons or Indians . . . I told you that last year."

"So you did," I replied.

As we stepped into the trading post, it smelled of harness

leather and gun oil. Quickly I made my purchases of trading items: knife blades, needles, and colorful beads . . . items that I could transport easily. I would have liked to purchase some cast-iron cookery as trade items, but settled for sheet-iron cookery, as cast iron was heavy.

I thought we were going to make our purchases and go, but Blue Star had other ideas. A born shopper, she looked at nearly everything in the store. At first Uncle tried to speed her along, but she snapped, "I want to see everything!" So, she saw everything.

While Blue Star shopped, Uncle and I passed the time. Across the street a hand pump squeaked, complaining, and you could hear water flowing into a metal bucket. A cow mooed, followed by the bark of a dog. Next door, a woman was hanging out her morning's wash.

A feisty miniature whirlwind caught the purple petals of tiny lilac flowers as they fell from a bush near the rear of the store. Giving them a dizzy swirl, the baby whirlwind dropped the petals in the dust. A blue jay lit on the edge of a watering trough, then lifted off again.

At last Blue Star emerged from the store with her treasures, which Uncle and I carefully packed on one of his calico ponies. All of Uncle's ponies were calico.

Mr. Poulsen seemed exhausted. "Take care," he muttered as we swung into our saddles. "Come back when you have more pelts to sell."

I was uneasy as we passed the saloon where I had seen Jacob Foster earlier in the day. Not that I was scared of him, but I had a healthy respect for the man, same as I have a healthy respect for the devil, Foster's master. All was quiet.

At the stables I stepped down, looking for Charlie. "Know where I can find Charlie Jones?" I asked a loafer.

"You just never mind Charlie Jones," a man growled as he

stepped from the harness room. It was Jacob Foster.

"We don't take kindly to Injuns or Injun lovers," he snapped, spitting the words from his lips.

"Hello Jacob," I said. "Fancy meeting you here. It's not like you to meet a man face to face. Your specialty is killing helpless women and children with infested blankets, isn't it?"

A sour grin spread across his face. "Ain't no law 'gainst killin' Injuns," he said. "As the saying goes, 'Mites make lice.'" He gave me a hard look, trying to stare me down, but failed and changed his tactic. "I hear tell you're one of Holy Joe's boys. They say you're a Harold. What name shall we put on your grave marker, 'Holy Joe Harold?'"

'Course Foster was referring to Joseph Smith, but if his intentions were to insult me, he failed. Yet I recalled Papa telling about the Kirtland days when Joseph's enemies were all calling him Holy Joe. Brigham Young had walked through the streets of Kirtland with a bull whip, defending the prophet.

"Suit yourself about the name, Jacob, but I'd say I'm more of a Brigham Harold than a Holy Joe Harold."

"You just get right back on your horse and hightail it out of town like a whipped puppy, Brigham, or get yourself a gun."

"Can't," I said. "The storekeeper said he can't sell guns to Mormons. Thought I might take yours."

Jacob didn't like it, he surely didn't. "Well then, boy," he said, on the verge of losing his temper, "I guess you'll just have to draw that knife at your waist. I'll give you 'til the count of three. When I say three, I'm gonna kill you."

"I wouldn't do that if I were you, Foster!" All eyes turned to three mountain men. "I know the kid," one of them said. "He has something of a reputation amongst the Pawnee . . . said to be blessed by the Great Spirit. The Pawnees believe it, and so do I."

"One!" shouted Foster, ignoring the mountain man. His voice was higher than it had been.

"Hold on," a bystander said. "You can't do that. He's not

armed!"

"Two!" Foster shouted, pretending he hadn't heard.

I pretended to scratch the back of my neck as my fingers closed around my throwing knife. As Foster's mouth was starting to form the word "three," my knife flashed to his forearm, passing clean through between the bone and tendons.

A man can get off a shot even if he has a knife in his forearm, using reflex action. So I made a quick jump to the left and drew my second knife. Foster's left hand grabbed for the knife in his arm, but his right hand continued to draw. As he drew he tried to cock his single-action revolver with his thumb, but on first try he couldn't master it. He didn't get a second try, 'cuz I kicked the pistol from his grasp.

"Well, I'll be," said a bystander. "The kid was faster with his knife than Foster was with his gun."

"I tried to tell him," the mountain man said.

I stepped to Foster's pistol where it lay in the dirt. Picking it up, I wiped the dust from it and slid it into my belt.

Foster was cursing as I relieved him of my knife, then broke into a fit of coughing. "I could have killed you, Foster," I said, "but vengeance belongs to God. Judging by your cough, you're dying. You're too sick to be gunning for people. Don't you have anyone to stand by you during your final days?"

"I don't need your damn sympathy," he snapped, a little weakly. "What about my revolver?"

"It's mine now, because I can't take the chance of you using your good hand to shoot me in the back as I leave."

"I don't shoot with my left arm."

"Then you won't need your weapon, as you'll likely not survive your cough long enough for your right arm to heal. Besides, it's an old Indian custom that to the victor belong the spoils."

I gave the bystanders a long, appraising look, but none seemed inclined to cause me any trouble. Still, I backed to my roan and swung into the saddle, keeping the bystanders in sight at all times.

"We'll ride along with you," the mountain man said, "in case anyone gets an idea it wasn't a fair fight." I nodded.

"Seen you once in the village, but I don't know your name," I said to one of the mountain men after we had traveled about a mile. "What do you want to be called?"

"Most folks call me Jedediah Johnson."

"Heard of you," I said. "The Indians call you 'Liver Eater.'"

"Yep, you heard of me, all right. Sometimes it pays to keep Indians a little scared of you, so I throw the fear of God into 'em now and again."

We parted at Westport, Uncle and I . . . a long embrace, then he and Blue Star rode away. In truth I almost rode with them, though he and Blue Star surely didn't need a white-eyes hanging around as Uncle reacquainted himself with his Sioux family.

It seemed like forever since the day I'd first met Uncle on the banks of the Missouri, and even longer since Mama and Papa had died that cold winter day in Missouri. I thought of Grandmother and White Rabbit, and my eyes started to grow hot, so I ducked my head.

It was best that I go with the mountain men and learn something about my own people, yet I sat on my horse and watched long and hard as Uncle and Blue Star rode north. The three mountain men waited patiently, knowing a lad needs time to say good-bye.

I watched Uncle and Blue Star until they were tiny in the distance. Then Uncle turned and waved, and very faintly I heard the familiar Pawnee war whoop.

ABOUT THE AUTHOR

Boyd Richards is a lively storyteller who helps his yarns come alive through vigorous research. Yet if the end result of a story doesn't move a reader closer to Christ, or at least to good works, he considers that story a failure.

Boyd says he does his best creative work while jogging. He is a marathon jogger, hiker, and backpacker. He says he used to consider himself a mountain man, but the Lord decided he should be a Scouter instead.

Raised in Utah and northern Arizona, Boyd filled a proselyting mission to the East Central States. Less than a year after his return, he accepted the call to serve for four and a half years as a full-time labor missionary.

Boyd and his wife, the former Margie Powell of Lehi, Utah, have five "homemade" sons and one "imported" son, an adopted Korean boy. With this large family of boys, Boyd and Margie are deeply involved in Scouting (both are Silver Beaver Scouters). All six sons are Eagle Scouts. The oldest three are returned missionaries, and the fourth is now serving a mission in Brazil.

A graduate of Brigham Young University, Boyd is employed as a security officer for The Church of Jesus Christ of Latter-day Saints. He is a stake missionary and serves in the Boy Scouts of America as Scout Vice-Chairman of the White Buffalo District.